LOVING DANIEL

Book One of Tucker's Landing Series

Lina Rehal

Loving Daniel
Loving Daniel Copyright © 2017 Lina Rehal
All rights reserved. No part of this text may be reproduced in any form without the express written permission of the author.
Published by Lina Rehal
Printed in the United States of America
Cover Photo: Perkins Cove by Lina Rehal
Author Photo: By Katie Martin
ISBN-10: 099761501X
ISBN-13: 9780997615012
Version 01.02.2017
DISCLAIMER: *Loving Daniel* is a work of fiction. Names, characters, places and incidents are either the product of the author's imagination or are used fictitiously. Any resemblance to actual persons, living or dead, or to actual events is entirely coincidental.
Contact Lina Rehal

Email: rehalcute@aol.com

Website: www.thefuzzypinkmuse.com

DEDICATION

*This book is for those who believe in love and second chances.
Never give up on your dreams.*

SPECIAL THANKS

Thank you to my beta readers, Christina Levine, Kathie Moulison and Jo Capano. I greatly appreciate the time and effort each of you put into reading *Loving Daniel*. Your comments and suggestions were a tremendous help in getting this story to its final draft.

To my husband, Dick Rehal, for encouraging me to finish this book and "get it out there."

To Gina Martin for helping with my research on PTSD and medical issues.

To Ralph Fanti for answering my many questions about the state of Maine.

A special thank you to my granddaughter, Katie Martin, for helping with the author photo.

Thanks to my two writing groups, North Shore Scribes and Red Rock Rewriters, for your critiques and encouragement.

OTHER BOOKS BY LINA REHAL

October In New York

Carousel Kisses

CONTENTS

Special Thanks		v
Chapter 1	Aidan	1
Chapter 2	Grace	4
Chapter 3	Aidan	11
Chapter 4	Jonathan	14
Chapter 5	In the Attic	16
Chapter 6	Grace Remembers	19
Chapter 7	Elise	21
Chapter 8	The Book Nook	25
Chapter 9	Jonathan In Albany	29
Chapter 10	Aidan	36
Chapter 11	Aidan Goes Inside	38
Chapter 12	Grace and Aidan Meet	40
Chapter 13	Charlene	45
Chapter 14	Lunch At Hattie's	50
Chapter 15	After Lunch	56
Chapter 16	Grace At the Hotel	58
Chapter 17	Aidan and Charlene	61
Chapter 18	Charlene and J B	64

Chapter 19	Dinner	66
Chapter 20	Call From Kelli	70
Chapter 21	Antiquity	72
Chapter 22	Flo's	78
Chapter 23	Ogunquit	80
Chapter 24	Perkins Cove	85
Chapter 25	The Blue Pitcher	91
Chapter 26	Jonathan's Phone Call	95
Chapter 27	Charlene's Message	98
Chapter 28	Grace In Casselton	100
Chapter 29	Kelli	106
Chapter 30	The swim	108
Chapter 31	At the Lake	113
Chapter 32	After the Loving	118
Chapter 33	Call From Jonathan	122
Chapter 34	Aidan Alone Again	124
Chapter 35	Grace At Home	126
Chapter 36	Lunch With Jonathan	133
Chapter 37	Elise and Jimmy	141
Chapter 38	Grace Tells Her Kids	145
Chapter 39	Call To Aidan	150
Chapter 40	Back To Maine	153
Chapter 41	Grace At Aidan's	155
Chapter 42	First Night At Aidan's	158
Chapter 43	Elise and Jonathan	162
Chapter 44	Friday At Aidan's	170
Chapter 45	Aidan's Nightmare	177
Chapter 46	Kelli and Grace	182
Chapter 47	At The Blue Anchor	191
Chapter 48	Grace Goes Home	196
Chapter 49	The Apology	199

Chapter 50	Donald	203
Chapter 51	Aidan Arrives	206
Chapter 52	Aidan Meets the Kids	213
Chapter 53	Elise, Brian and Jimmy	218
Chapter 54	Dinner At The Black Rock	220
Chapter 55	At the Cemetery	224
Chapter 56	Grace Finds Out	231
Chapter 57	Preparing For the Cookout	235
Chapter 58	Fireworks	241
Chapter 59	Grace and Elise	247
Chapter 60	Aidan and Donald	250
Chapter 61	The Cookout	253
Chapter 62	Aidan and Elise	259
Chapter 63	The Wrap Up	263
Chapter 64	Breakfast	268

Worth Waiting For		275
Chapter 1	Jonathan	277
About the Author		281

"Believe in your dreams.
Follow them. Reach for them.
Make them happen."
Lina Rehal

CHAPTER 1
AIDAN

When Aidan woke up, he found himself in the living room. It was dark. He could see the full moon through the open blinds. The TV was in sleep mode. Red numbers from a digital clock on the end table glared at him. 2 a.m. *Must have nodded off on the sofa again*, he thought.

He had been dreaming. But, this time was different. He didn't wake up in a panic or soaked from sweat. It wasn't one of his usual nightmares. Aidan couldn't remember this one, but he wanted to. It was about something, or someone pleasant. He was sure of that. Yet, it left him with a sense of sadness or loss.

The dream bothered him. He closed his eyes for a few minutes, hoping it would come back to him. When it didn't, he decided to get up and go to bed. Swinging his long legs off the sofa, Aidan stood up. The book he had been reading slid off his chest and fell to the floor. The cover gave him a jolt. *Loving Daniel* by Grace Madden. He picked it up, sat down and remembered.

Aidan had been dreaming about Grace Devlin, a woman he fell in love with back in the late 1980's in Massachusetts. She was in college then, studying to be a journalist. He was working at a local garage and taking business administration courses at night. They met when her car broke down and Aidan had to tow it back to the garage. She was a petite, beautiful young girl with long, flowing hair the color of copper and eyes as green as emeralds in the right light. He gave her a ride home that day and invited her to dinner before she got out of his truck.

In the dream, she was the Grace he knew back then. She was vibrant, tenacious, impatient and crazy in love with him. It was coming back to him. He had been kissing her. Awake now, Aidan could still feel the softness of her lips on his and smell the traces of lemon shampoo in her hair. It felt real. It felt right. He wanted to go back to sleep so he could hold her and tell her he loved her.

The sad feeling grew stronger, as he began to recall the last part of the dream. They were arguing about something. That wasn't like them. She was angry with him. He could see the hurt in her eyes. Her voice sounded exactly as it did twenty-four years ago. She was crying and saying the same things she said to him then. It ended with her pleading with him like she did the night he destroyed their hopes of a future together.

Aidan switched on a lamp. He thumbed through the pages of the book until he found the chapter he was looking for. He leaned back against the pillows and read it again.

Daniel and Abby were standing in the gazebo in her back yard. It was raining. He had taken her there so they would be out of earshot from the house, in case her parents came home.

"Why are you doing this, Daniel? I love you. Did I do something wrong?"

He couldn't look at her. "It's not you, Abby, it's me."

"But, there must be a reason. You don't just break up with someone for no reason. Don't you love me anymore?"

Daniel couldn't tell her why he was breaking up with her. "I'll always love you, Abby, but things are different now. I'm different now."

"No you're not. You're the same person you were before you went away. The same person I fell in love with. If you still loved me, you wouldn't do this. Damn you, Daniel. I deserve better than this!"

Aidan began to understand his sad feelings. He thumbed through the pages until finding where he left off before falling asleep. He had to finish the last few chapters, even though he had a pretty good idea how it ended.

CHAPTER 2
GRACE

Grace woke up an hour before her alarm clock was due to go off. She was excited and nervous about her first book signing for her latest romance novel. *Why am I nervous? I've done hundreds of these. Reviewers say Loving Daniel is the best love story I've ever written. I can't sleep. I might as well get up.* She slipped on a robe and went downstairs.

The clock on the microwave read 7:15. The house was quiet. Elise had already gone to work. Jimmy was away at school. Grace dropped a K-cup in the coffee maker and popped a slice of bread in the toaster. *Maybe it's spending a few days in Maine with Jonathan I'm worried about. I know our relationship is purely platonic, but there's no one I'd rather spend time with. I'm just being silly. No reason to feel this way.*

Grace thought about Jonathan Blake as she sipped her coffee. He was the one who arranged tomorrow's event. She met the well-known author with the movie-star looks twelve years ago when her husband invited him to dinner. Jonathan was one of Jim's clients. He had just moved to Tucker's Landing from Albany. The women thought his bedroom eyes and boyish grin made him look sexy and vulnerable. They loved having him as a neighbor.

Jonathan became Jim's best friend. He and Grace considered him family. After Jim's passing, he was a great comfort to all of them, especially Grace. She stopped writing for close to a year. If it hadn't been for his encouragement and patience, she might never have written another book. Over the past three years, next to her girlfriend Valerie, he'd become her closest friend and confidant.

When he set up the event at the Book Nook in Whittier, Jonathan suggested they spend a few days in Maine together. He wanted to take her to his favorite seafood restaurant. "You'll love the lobster in this place."

Grace was afraid he secretly held out hope for a romantic relationship with her, even though she made it clear they could be nothing more than good friends. "I love you, Jonathan, but not the way you want me to. I don't want to risk losing what we have."

It made her feel better that he didn't seem disappointed when she reminded him to book separate rooms. "You're right. No need to add fuel to the rumor mill. But, two friends can still enjoy a little mini-vacation. We've earned it."

She was about to go upstairs to shower, when the phone rang.

"Hey, Grace. Are you ready to wow them in Maine?"

"Hey yourself, J B. I sure am. I have to pack and eat lunch. Oh, and I need to call Charlene to confirm the time we'll be starting and make sure there aren't any last minute glitches."

Jonathan was always one step ahead of her. "No problem. I spoke to her this morning. She has plenty of books and a table. We can just walk in and set up."

"I swear you're the most organized person in the whole writing world."

"I was a Boy Scout before I became a writer."

"By the way, Charlene's been getting a lot of good response from the press release in their local paper."

"That's great. I hope we have a good turnout."

"She said some guy called asking about you. He asked about Grace Devlin and then corrected himself and said he meant Madden."

Grace wondered who would use her maiden name. "That's odd. My readers don't know me as Devlin. What if he's some kook?"

Jonathan didn't want to let her know it, but he thought it was strange too. "Maybe it was someone who knew you before you were married. I wouldn't worry about it. He probably won't show up. "

Grace couldn't help being concerned. "I doubt I have many male readers. Maybe that's why I've had this strange feeling all morning."

"What feeling?"

"Like something bad is about to happen."

"I'll be there the whole time to keep an eye on things. Finish your packing and have lunch. Is one-thirty okay to pick you up? I'd like to be on the road by two."

"Thanks again, Jonathan, for suggesting me to Charlene. See you when you get here."

Grace made sure everything she needed was in one of the boxes stacked by the front door. "Let's see," she said out loud. "A cloth for the table, banner, pens, business cards, bookmarks, two posters and some extra books in case the store runs out."

Satisfied things were in order, she went upstairs to shower and get dressed.

When she came out of the shower, the phone was ringing. Wrapped in a towel, Grace hurried to the bedroom to answer it.

"Glad I caught you. Something's come up."

Jonathan sounded upset. "What is it? Is something wrong?"

"It's my dad. They think he's had a heart attack."

"Oh, no."

"I'm going to have to leave for Albany right away. I won't be able to go to Maine. I'm sorry. I hate to disappoint you."

"Don't worry about me. You need to be with your family. Is there anything I can do?"

"You could call the hotel and cancel my reservation. I'll call or text you later."

"I'll take care of it. Keep in touch."

Grace stood in the middle of her room. Cold and wet, she started shaking. *I knew something was going to happen. Poor Jonathan. I hope his dad pulls through.*

After she dried herself off and got dressed, Grace sat on the side of the bed for several minutes trying to figure out what to do. *I can handle the book signing alone. What about the vacation? I suppose I'd better cancel my room too. Or, should I? I could use a few days to myself.*

She pulled her suitcase out of the closet, tossed it on the bed and began filling it with clothes and enough toiletries for the next several days. As she packed, Grace thought about the two men she had loved in her lifetime.

Jim Madden was a successful attorney, specializing in real estate. He was a kind, generous man who always made time for his family. He was the one person Grace could count on, no matter what. Jim was there for her during those dark days after Aidan left when she had no one else to turn to.

She dated him in high school. He was personable, good-looking and extremely intelligent. With his six foot two solid build, he was a star of the basketball team. The girls loved his electric blue eyes. He could have dated anyone he wanted, but the only girl Jim Madden wanted was Grace Devlin. He followed her around like a puppy.

She enjoyed Jim's company. He was a sweet, thoughtful boy who made her laugh. They didn't talk much about their future or what would happen after graduation. He just assumed they would get married after college, but she hoped to be a journalist and travel.

Jim was accepted to Yale. With him going to school in Connecticut and Grace in Boston, their relationship suffered. Grace met someone else. When Jim came home at Thanksgiving, she was dating a young man who graduated a year ahead of them in high school.

Aidan McRae was different from anyone she had ever known. He was smart, logical and independent. Grace liked that about him. She had a hard time making decisions and often asked for his advice. He made her laugh.

Aidan worked as a mechanic in a local garage to help pay for his education. He went to school at night. He liked working with his hands and could fix anything. Slightly over six feet tall, he had broad shoulders and strong muscular arms from working out. His short black hair curled at the ends when he needed a haircut. Grace loved the touch of blue around the edges of his stone gray eyes.

When Jim came home at Christmas, Grace told him she was in love with Aidan. She knew how it hurt Jim and hated doing that to him, but couldn't help the way she felt.

For two years, Grace and Aidan were inseparable. They went to college dances, frat parties and studied together at the Library. When he wasn't working at the garage, they went to the movies or bowling. In the summer, they went to the beach. Sometimes they cuddled on the glider on Grace's front porch or sat in the gazebo in her back yard and planned their future.

Aidan wanted to get married after Grace graduated from college. "Let's get married as soon as you graduate."

Grace wanted to marry him more than anything, but she still had dreams of becoming a journalist. "Shouldn't I get a job first?"

"I guess that would be a good idea."

He wanted a big family. "How many children do you think we should have?"

"One thing at a time," she told him.

"I'd like four, but we can negotiate."

Grace had no qualms about marrying Aidan. In her diary, she wrote, "He believes in me and encourages me to write and to be myself. With him, I know it's possible to have marriage, a family and a career."

Then Aidan joined the Marines and everything changed.

She remembered the day he told her he had enlisted. "You did what?"

"I enlisted in the Marines."

"Without even discussing it with me? How could you do that? What about us? Our plans? Our future?"

"I did it for us. It's a way for me to get my education without having to work at the garage and go to school nights. At the rate I'm going, it will take way too long before I can start a business of my own and support a family."

"But, there's so much trouble in the world. You'll have to go away. You could end up in the Middle East."

Even now, when she thinks about Aidan, Grace remembers how much she loved him and is filled with mixed emotions. She wonders why he ended it between them with no explanation.

The pain has dissipated over the years, but not her memories. Despite what he did to her, she has always saved a place in her heart for him. Hidden in some crevice in the back of her mind, Grace keeps the hope she will someday find out what his reasons were. Maybe then she can forgive him.

CHAPTER 3
AIDAN

Aidan finally put the book out of his mind and went to bed. It was close to 4:30. He drifted off to sleep with thoughts of Grace lying next to him. He imagined her long, red hair spread across the pillow and could feel the warmth of her body up against his. He wanted to pull her closer to him, but knew if he tried to touch her, she'd vanish. His fantasy of her would turn back into reality.

Aidan's internal alarm clock woke him up at his usual time of 6 a.m. Knowing he couldn't go to work on only an hour and a half of sleep, he called Sam, his assistant at the hardware store.

"Sorry to call so early, Sam, but something's come up. I won't be in until after lunch."

Sam Cross had worked for Aidan since he opened the hardware store nearly twenty years ago. He knew better than to ask too many questions. Aidan was a good boss and treated him well. Sam loved him like a son. In his early sixties, he liked working and had no intention of retiring any too soon. "Take as long as you need. I can handle things."

"I know you can. Thanks. I'll see you in a few hours."

Aidan rolled over and fell into a deep sleep. He didn't wake up until he heard his cell phone ringing at 10:55. He reached over and grabbed it off the nightstand. His daughter's number came up.

He tried to sound awake. "Mornin' Kelli."

"Dad? Are you okay? You sound like I woke you up. Why aren't you at work?"

The last thing Aidan needed today was his daughter mothering him. "I'm fine, Kel. Just tired. Needed to catch up on some sleep. I was about to hop in the shower and go to work when the phone rang."

His daughter wondered what would make him so tired he'd go to work late. That wasn't like him. Ne never missed work. Not even when he was depressed.

"I won't keep you then. I was just calling to say hi. You didn't answer your cell phone earlier so I called the store. When Sam said you weren't in today, I got worried."

Kelli was overprotective of Aidan. She lost her mother at the age of six in a car accident. Since then, it had been just the two of them. He understood why she did this and loved that his daughter watched out for him, but sometimes Kelli crossed over the line. She knew he needed his space and was usually pretty good about it, but if there was a hint of anything wrong, she was all over him.

"Thanks, Sweetheart. We'll talk later."

Kelli knew her father was trying to hide something from her. *Just going into the shower, my foot. It's eleven o'clock and I woke him up. Who does he think he's fooling?* She slipped her phone back into her pocket and tried to get back to work.

Aidan got out of bed and went into the shower. He made a mental note to call Kelli later. He didn't want her knowing he was up until after 4 a.m. thinking about the past and dwelling on his regrets. How could he explain reading a romance book, written by the only woman he ever loved, to his daughter?

CHAPTER 4
JONATHAN

Jonathan Blake knew in his gut he would someday become an author. It didn't come easy. He accumulated his share of rejections before selling his first novel and becoming successful. His passion for writing kept him from getting discouraged.

He started out writing short stories and personal essays, submitting his work to magazines and periodicals. Although his work was published on occasion, it wasn't anything he could live on. With the help of a good connection or two, he landed a job working as a reporter on the city desk at a newspaper in Albany, New York, where he grew up. He shortened his name to J B Blake and began using it as his pen name.

In less than a year, the paper offered Jonathan a position as a theater critic and gave him his own column. People who enjoyed the theater respected his opinions. Those who received favorable reviews invited him to after show parties where he met agents and other writers.

With his charm and personality, he fit right into the theater crowd. Women vied for the attention of the handsome, six-foot-two writer with the smoldering eyes. He dated several of them, but never for long. Between his job and working on his writing career, he had no time for a romantic relationship. At least, not until he met Nicole King, the beautiful, young actress whose first leading role he reviewed.

His job paid the bills, but it wasn't what he wanted to do. Jonathan wanted to write books. He got up at five in the morning so he could write for a couple of hours before going to work at the paper.

After several rejections, one of his fiction stories was published in a literary magazine. He was asked to submit another. He was finally beginning to feel like a writer.

It took him two years to complete his first novel and another year to find a publisher. *Murder at Pine Lake* didn't make any best-seller lists, but it did well enough to get his name out there. His publisher offered him an advance on his next book. It marked the beginning of his career as a crime writer. His third book, *Kill the Messenger,* made the list. Over the next few years, J B Blake became a top selling author known for his murder mysteries. He had two books on the best-seller list by the age of thirty-five. Jonathan Bentley Blake was finally doing what he had always wanted to do.

CHAPTER 5
IN THE ATTIC

Dust motes swirled through the stale air as Grace wiped a rag over the old mahogany hope chest that had once belonged to her grandmother. She sneezed several times before attempting to open it. *Guess it's been a while since I've been up here.*

Grace had ventured into the attic to look for family photo albums. Her cousin, Lucille, lost a lot of pictures when she moved to Florida. "I'd love to have a few of us when we were kids. If you could scan some and email them to me, I'd really appreciate it."

"I'm sure I have plenty up in the attic. I'll see what I can find."

When she pushed open the lid, the strong scent of cedar brought back memories of her childhood and her grandmother. "What's that smell? Why do you keep things in that box?"

Her grandmother laughed. "The smell is cedar. It keeps my nice tablecloths and crocheted doilies from getting eaten by moths. Someday, I'll give it to your mother and she'll give it to you."

"What would I keep in it?"

"Things you want to save for your grandchildren, like my silver tea set or photo albums. Special possessions you might want to look back at and remember about. Maybe a scrapbook or a diary."

"What's in the blue box?"

Her grandmother took the box out and held it to her heart. "Letters from your grandfather. He wrote them when he was in the Army. Every now and then, I like to read them again."

Grace liked the idea of having a special hiding place for things she didn't want anyone to know about. "If I ever have letters from someone I love, I'll keep mine in here, too."

Grace pulled out a few family albums and scrapbooks. She smiled at the pictures of her parents when they were young and laughed at the hairdos and funny clothes. *Lucille will like these, I'm sure.*

When she was done looking at photos, she dug down further into the chest to see if there was anything else she might want to show her cousin. Next to the silver tea set, under a bag of doilies and a stack of letters, Grace found the blue velvet box. *The special things I saved to look back at and remember about.*

Running her fingers over the faded velvet, she opened the box and let the memories out. Each item brought back a special event or time in her life before everything changed forever. There was a picture of her holding a stuffed giraffe Aidan won at the Topsfield Fair. He had to shoot out a big red star with a rifle. It was almost impossible to win, but he was good at it. The man didn't like it, but people were watching and he had to give him the prize.

She found ticket stubs from a Christmas play he took her to and the friendship ring she had long since forgotten. She remembered the night he gave her the gold ring with the two open diamond hearts. "Someday, I'll get you a ring with diamonds you can see."

There were several dried-up roses pressed between wrinkled pieces of waxed paper. Aidan was always giving her roses. Yellow ones were her favorite. On special occasions, he gave her one beautiful red rose surrounded by five yellow ones. He couldn't afford a dozen.

There were other pictures of the two of them and one of Aidan in his uniform. It was taken before he went to Iraq. She always wondered why he broke up with her without an explanation or reason. Maybe if she had known why, it would have made the break-up easier somehow.

Grace had almost forgotten what else she tucked away until she saw the pale yellow ribbon wrapped around her journal and Aidan's letters. She untied the bow and opened the book.

Reading about Aidan brought the pain back to the surface. She never stopped loving him. Even when she married Jim, Grace still had feelings for the young man who towed her car to the garage and gave her a ride home that day so long ago.

Grace returned the blue box to the bottom of the chest. She took the journal and Aidan's letters to her office, where she continued to read them. As the memories came flooding back, an idea for a book formed in her head. *Maybe if I write our story, it will finally give me closure.*

CHAPTER 6
GRACE REMEMBERS

Curled up on the overstuffed chair in her office, reading Aidan's old letters and her long since forgotten journal, Grace lost track of the time. She glanced at her watch. *Five-thirty. No wonder my stomach is growling.*

Not wanting to break away from the memories just yet, she closed her eyes and let her thoughts drift back to those days of innocence. The days before her hopes and dreams were shattered and her life changed forever. Grace thought about the two young people so desperately in love before they were torn apart by something she never understood.

AMR Loves GD 4ever. Aidan carved it in the old oak tree in her back yard. The memory of it came back as if it had happened yesterday. She could almost hear his voice.

"Just in case anyone ever doubts it."

"I believe it," she told him. "That's all that matters."

"Promise me you'll always believe it."

"I promise."

More than anyone, Aidan encouraged her to write. "You're a good writer, Grace. You have a lot of potential. Someday, I'll read your books."

"Don't you think you might be a bit biased?"

"Not at all. I knew you had talent before I fell in love with you."

"Do you really think I might write a book someday, Aidan?"

"You can do anything you want to, Gracie. Don't ever give up on your dreams."

He repeated the same words in one of his letters.

The more Grace remembered about the young man who taught her to believe in herself, the more compelled she became to write their story.

Using passages from her journal, his letters and her own memories, she created Daniel Sheridan and Abby Maguire to tell the story she kept inside of her for over two decades. She told no one. Not even her two best friends, Valerie and Jonathan, were aware *Loving Daniel* was a fictionalized version of a love she once knew.

CHAPTER 7
ELISE

Elise looked forward to having the house to herself. She hadn't signed up for any summer art courses and was taking time off from her job at the gallery. Her brother wouldn't be home from school until the weekend. Her mother was at a book event and taking a mini-vacation in Maine for a few days. Elise planned to enjoy the peace and quiet while she could. *It'll be nice to hang around in slippers and sweats and not have her questioning my every move. She's been on my case a lot lately. She seems to forget I'm an adult. Maybe a little shopping and relaxation will do her some good.*

She retreated to the den with her morning coffee. Comfortable in what used to be her father's favorite chair, she picked up the remote and started flipping channels.

Elise was happy her mom decided not to cancel her vacation when Jonathan's dad got sick and he had to back out at the last minute. She was probably more disappointed than her mother that he couldn't go. Elise adored him. She thought he was perfect for Grace and secretly hoped there was more to their relationship than they let on. The one time she brought it up, Grace quickly dismissed it.

"Mom, you need someone in your life and you have so much in common with Jonathan. Anyone can see he's in love with you."

"Jonathan and I are good friends. We like things the way they are."

She never mentioned it again, but when they were going away together, Elise couldn't help thinking things might change.

By noon, she was tired of sitcoms and playing games on her iPad. She answered two text messages from her mom. The first was to let her know she had arrived in Maine. The second one was to tell her the signing was going well and that an anonymous fan sent her roses. Elise thought that was a bit strange since most of her mother's fans were women. She wondered if they were from Jonathan, but didn't dare to even suggest it. *I wouldn't be surprised, though. He's so thoughtful.*

Just as Elise was about to make a sandwich, her phone pinged. She laughed at Brian's message.

Are you bored yet? Want company tonight? I'll bring pizza.

The tall, sandy-haired star of his college basketball team could be stubborn at times, but he was also sweet, thoughtful and fun to be with. She'd been dating Brian O'Leary for the past five years. It hadn't always been an easy relationship. Elise could be difficult and moody. He was wonderful and understanding when she lost her dad. Lately, their relationship had been becoming more serious. She wasn't sure about her feelings on that.

Make it pepperoni and it's a date.

After lunch, she put on a hat and sunscreen and took a nap by the pool. When she woke up, it was 2:30. She sent her mom a text, but got no reply. *Maybe she's driving. I'll check with her in a while. Guess I'll go online and look at some fall courses.*

Elise spent an hour on her laptop doing research. When she found the information and tried to print it out, the printer was out of paper. *Mom must have extra paper in her office. She won't mind if I take some.*

Grace's office was neat and organized, unlike when she was working on a book and papers were everywhere. The computer was off. A copy of *Loving Daniel* and a stack of bookmarks were on the desk.

Elise walked over to the printer. The paper tray was empty. She opened the supply closet. There were only two reams left. She took one out, filled the tray and kept a little for herself. Wanting to let her mother know she needed to buy more, Elise went to the desk to look for something to write on. She found a pen, wrote a message on a sticky note and stuck it on the monitor.

When Elise got up to leave, she noticed a piece of paper under the desk. She pushed the chair back and picked it up. The paper was faded. Its edges were worn. *It looks like an old letter. Must be something she was using for a book. I wonder which one?* As she leaned the letter against the monitor, she couldn't help seeing some of the words.

"I miss you. I miss sitting in the gazebo planning our future."

Wait a minute. This sounds familiar. Didn't Abby and Daniel sit in a Gazebo and do that? Did she use this in Loving Daniel?

Thinking it was something Grace used for a book, Elise unfolded the letter. It was dated 1991 and had smudges in spots that looked like water marks.

"Dear Gracie, I love you and miss you more than I can say...."

Dear Gracie? Gazebo? Elise remembered the gazebo in her grandmother's back yard. *This is a love letter written to my mom. She used it in her book. But, who wrote it?* She turned it over and read the signature. 4ever, Aidan.

Elise didn't read the whole letter. Once she realized it was written to her mother, she couldn't. She didn't feel right reading her mother's personal mail. But, she read enough to know the man who wrote it is Daniel. But, who was Aidan? And why would she write about him now?

Elise put the letter back under the desk. She went back to her room, took out her copy of *Loving Daniel* and headed for the den.

CHAPTER 8
THE BOOK NOOK

Grace arrived at The Book Nook forty-five minutes before the scheduled time of the event. She had no trouble finding the small bookstore in the center of town. She pulled into the designated lot behind it and walked around to the front door. A slender blonde woman, who appeared to be in her mid to late forties, greeted her.

"Good morning, Grace. I'm Charlene Carter. We've spoken on the phone several times. So nice to finally meet you."

"It's nice to meet you too. Your store is charming. Thank you so much for inviting me."

"It's my pleasure. I've been a fan of yours for a long time. We sell a lot of your books. I just finished reading *Loving Daniel*. I couldn't put it down. I have it in the back room. When you have a minute, I'd like you to sign it."

"I'm glad you enjoyed it. I'd be happy to."

Charlene seemed disappointed about Jonathan's absence. "I was looking forward to seeing J B. He speaks highly of you. As you know, he's had several author events here himself. It's such a shame he couldn't be here. Too bad about his dad."

"He thinks a lot of you as well. I was thrilled when he said you were interested in having me as a guest author. I wish he could have been here too, but his place is with his family."

"Of course. Let me introduce you to Lexi, my assistant. Then I'll show you where to set up and we'll help you carry in your things."

Grace followed her to the register, where a petite brunette, a little younger than Charlene, was tagging books.

"Grace, this is Lexi Stone, my Assistant Manager. Lexi, meet Grace Madden, our guest author for today."

Lexi's pretty hazel eyes, accented by purple shadow and eyeliner, lit up when she smiled. She brushed the thick brown curls away from her face before taking Grace's hand. "Welcome to The Book Nook. I've been looking forward to meeting you."

"Thank you. It's nice to meet you."

"Lexi's my right arm. If I'm busy and you need something, feel free to ask her. Come on. I'll show you where you'll be sitting."

Charlene led Grace to a square wooden table toward the back of the store. "It may seem a little out of the way, but you will be highly visible and, as you can see, we have good signage. I think we have enough books on hand."

Grace couldn't help noticing the roses in the center of the table. "This will be fine. I have extra books in my car, just in case. The roses are beautiful. Do you do that for all your author events?"

Charlene had neglected to mention the special delivery. "What? Oh, I'm sorry. I forgot. Those came for you this morning. I had nothing to do with it."

"For me?"

"Yes. I had just unlocked the door when the florist showed up. One absolutely gorgeous red rose surrounded by five of the prettiest yellow ones I've ever seen. No name on the card. Looks to me like you have an admiring fan."

Grace looked at the blank card. "It was probably Jonathan."

Charlene looked a bit surprised. "Oh? I'm sorry if I said something I shouldn't have. I didn't realize you and J B had that kind of relationship."

Grace thought Charlene looked relieved when she clarified her comment. "Oh, no. It's okay. We're just good friends."

In her book, Daniel sent Abby yellow roses with one red rose in the middle. The only two men who sent her yellow roses were Jim and Aidan. Jim usually sent a mix of red and yellow. Aidan was the only one who sent her a half dozen with a red one in the center. Jonathan knew Daniel sent them to Abby that way in her book, but he didn't know where she got the idea. It would have been like him to send her flowers since he couldn't be there.

Charlene helped Grace carry in two of the three boxes, leaving the one with the books in the car. It didn't take her long to set up. She covered the table with a blue cloth, attached her banner across the front, set a hardcover copy of *Loving Daniel* on a stand, put out business cards, bookmarks, pens, a sheet for her fans to write their names and email addresses and two stacks of books to sign. Charlene brought out another small table so she could have the roses near her, but not in the way of customers.

People drifted in. The ones who didn't know about the event were curious when they saw the sign out front and wandered over. Those who were there specifically to meet Grace went directly to her table.

"I love your books, Ms. Madden. I came to have you sign my copy of *Loving Daniel* and to get one for a friend."

"I'd be happy to sign it for you."

The woman pointed to the roses. "Those are lovely. Just like Daniel would send."

The odd feeling Grace had the day before came back. *Aren't they though?*

CHAPTER 9
JONATHAN IN ALBANY

Jonathan sat quietly in his father's hospital room waiting for the doctor to come talk to the family. He listened to the slow, steady beeping of the monitor, ready to summon help at the slightest change in rhythm. A nurse came in to replace the bag of IV fluids.

"The doctor will be in soon. I'm right outside if you need anything."

"Thank you."

Henry Blake was a prominent leader of the community who believed in giving back. He liked helping people and enjoyed his family. Jonathan couldn't stand seeing the strong, independent man he loved and respected his whole life having to rely on others. As far as he knew, his father took good care of himself. Someone who ate healthy and worked out three times a week wasn't supposed to have a heart attack.

Jonathan watched his mother maintain her vigil. Ruth Blake would never want her family to know how worried she was, but he could see it in her eyes. The woman who always gave her children unconditional love and reassurance was going to need their comfort and support now. He wished his sister would hurry up and get there.

Jonathan checked his messages. Grace hadn't texted him since she arrived in Maine earlier that morning. Although he told her not to worry, Jonathan was concerned about the strange phone call from the man who asked for Grace Devlin. When he spoke to Charlene today, she asked if he was the one who sent the roses. He wondered who sent them and why. *What if it was the guy who called? What if Grace is right and he is a kook?* It all seemed odd.

He thought about how close they had become over the past few years, especially, the last two. When Jim died, Jonathan did as much as he could for Grace and the kids. Being there for them helped him deal with the loss of his friend.

After her kids went back to work and school, he noticed Grace had not re-scheduled any of her speaking engagements and avoided social events whenever possible. Worst of all, she stopped writing. She needed to get her life and career back on track. He encouraged her to get out of the house as much as he could.

"Grace, I'm speaking at a local book club tonight. Why don't you come along?"

"I've got some work to do. Maybe next time."

He knew it was an excuse. "Are you working on a new book?"

"No, not exactly."

Jonathan wasn't giving up that easily. "Then what's so important it can't wait until tomorrow? It would do you good to get out and I'd love to have you there."

"I'm just not ready yet."

"I miss my writing buddy. I could use a familiar face in the crowd. I'd do it for you."

She knew what he was trying to do. "You've been such a good friend to us, Jonathan. I can't refuse you a favor. Okay. I'll go."

A few weeks later, she helped him host a party for the launching of his latest novel. It was a start.

Jonathan spent a lot of time with Grace that first year. They went to dinner, movies, the theater and attended several book related events. He had hoped being around bookstores and authors would motivate her to write again, but it didn't seem to be working. After almost a year, she still hadn't written a word.

One night, at a party for a mutual author friend of theirs, they ran into Bradley Dunbar, a literary agent they knew.

"If it isn't Grace Madden and J B Blake. Nice to see you."

"Hey, Brad. How are you?" Jonathan asked.

"Hello, Bradley," said Grace.

"I'm doing okay. Just got back from six weeks in London." He looked at Grace. "How are you doing?"

"I'm fine, thank you."

Bradley seemed particularly interested in Grace. Jonathan figured he was trying to find out if she was writing another book. "Congratulations, J B I hear you recently released another Captain Carlisle book. What about you Grace? I haven't seen anything new from you in quite some time now. Can we expect to see something in the near future?"

Grace hesitated before she answered. "I'm working on it."

"I'm sure your readers will be happy about that. It was good seeing both of you."

Jonathan wondered why Grace gave Bradley Dunbar the idea she had something in the works. As soon as the agent was out of earshot, he asked her about it.

"Dunbar was certainly interested in you."

"I think he was trying to find out about us."

Jonathan wasn't sure what she was getting at. "You mean he wants to know if we're an item."

"Exactly."

They both laughed. "And I thought he was trying to get you as a client. Is that why you led him to believe you have a book in the works? To throw him off the track?"

"Partly."

That made Jonathan curious. "What do you mean?"

"I wanted to keep him wondering. I've been journaling again, so it wasn't a total lie."

"Glad to hear it."

"An idea has been swirling around in the back of my mind. Now, if I can only get something on paper."

"I'm even happier to hear that. You know, Grace, Jim wouldn't want you to waste your talent."

"I know. I'll write again, when the timing is right."

Jonathan didn't press for details. Knowing she wanted to write was enough.

Several weeks later, he went to New York on business. Returning home earlier than expected, he decided to drop by and invite Grace to dinner. She seemed pleased to see him. He remembered how pretty she looked standing in the doorway.

"Jonathan. When did you get back?"

"A couple hours ago. I wanted to surprise you. Have you had dinner yet?"

"No. I was just about to make myself something. Come in. How was New York?"

"Have dinner with me and I'll tell you."

Grace laughed. "That beats the sandwich I was going to offer you. Give me fifteen minutes."

During dinner, Jonathan filled her in on his trip and the meetings with his publisher in New York.

"All in all, the new book is doing great. We discussed my current work in progress."

"Another Captain Carlisle?"

"No. I'm working on something else. Enough about me. What's been going on with you this past two weeks?"

"Jimmy came home for a weekend. We all went out to dinner. I enjoyed having both kids around."

When he took her home, Grace invited him in. She led him into the living room. "Would you like coffee or a glass of wine?"

"No thanks. I'm all set."

"Have a seat. Now, I have a surprise for you. I'll be right back."

He sat patiently, waiting and wondering what she was up to. When she returned, Grace handed him a large thick manila envelope.

"What's this?"

"A manuscript."

"You've written a new book?"

"It's a very rough first draft. I'd like you to read it and tell me what you think."

He loved seeing that creative spark in her eyes again. "That's wonderful, Grace. Of course I'll read it."

He placed the manuscript on the coffee table, stood up and gave her a long, lingering hug.

Jonathan's thoughts about Grace were interrupted when the door opened and his sister entered the hospital room. A man, he guessed to be in his mid-forties, walked in after her.

Amanda brushed by Jonathan without acknowledging his presence. "Oh, good. Dad, you're awake. This is Dr. Vincent. We met at the nurses' station."

Jonathan didn't mind that Amanda ignored him. He was used to her grand entrances. He slipped his phone in his pocket and stood up.

"I'm Dr. Ralph Vincent, the surgeon Dr. Goldstein spoke to you about. How are you feeling today, Mr. Blake?"

"I've been better. This is my wife Ruth."

Jonathan introduced himself and shook the doctor's hand. "I'm Jonathan Blake. Thank you for coming. Can you tell us anything more about my father's condition?"

The doctor looked down at the chart he held in his hands. Before answering, he addressed Henry directly. "Is it all right with you, Mr. Blake, if I discuss this in front of your family?"

"Of course."

Dr. Vincent continued. "I've looked over your test results and gone over everything with Dr. Goldstein. I want to run one other test. Then I should have some better answers for you. I'll be back once I know more."

When Dr. Vincent left the room, Amanda turned toward her brother. "Can we get a cup of coffee?"

His younger sister didn't often show her vulnerable side. When she did, he was always the one who could calm her. "Sounds good. Dad, you rest. We'll be back."

They walked in silence to the coffee shop. Jonathan told her to have a seat while he got the coffee.

When he came back and sat down, Amanda spoke. "I'm sorry I blew past you like that back in the room. I'm really glad to see you."

"That's okay. I know you're upset."

"It's just hitting me how serious this is. I'm very worried, Jonathan."

Amanda was a lot like their dad. She was a strong woman and used to being in charge. It was difficult seeing her on the verge of falling apart, but he knew she needed him. He'd do whatever he could to help his sister. Jonathan reached across the table and covered her hand with is. "I know, Honey. We all are."

CHAPTER 10
AIDAN

Sitting in his truck, outside of the bookstore, Aidan fought the urge to ditch the whole idea and go back home. *What am I even doing here? I'm the last person she needs to see.*

He glanced down at the book on the seat next to him. Reading it had brought back bittersweet memories of a love he once knew and the woman he had never been able to forget. Questions filled his head.

Is Daniel Sheridan a fictitious character in a book or someone from Grace Madden's past? Is it the story of Abby and Daniel or Grace and Aidan? She changed the names and gave it a happy ending, but it's us. I know it's about us. There are too many similarities to be coincidence.

His mouth suddenly went dry. *What if I'm wrong? What if Loving Daniel has nothing to do with me? Maybe I just want it to be about me. If I'm not careful, I'll work myself into an anxiety attack.*

He wanted to see her. He had to find out. *Is there a message in her writing, or am I reading too much between the lines?*

Taking a deep breath, Aidan tried to calm himself. He pulled the bottle of water out of the cup holder and took a drink. *But, why, after all these years, would she write about us?* Aidan had to know the answers.

His heart raced at the thought of her. He wondered if Grace had figured out who sent the roses and how she'd react to seeing him again. Would she even recognize him?

Aidan got out of the truck, slid his sunglasses back down over his eyes, grabbed the book and walked across the street.

CHAPTER 11
AIDAN GOES INSIDE

Aidan saw her sitting at the back of the store as soon as he stepped inside. The sunlight, coming through the window, caught the copper color of her hair. She was wearing it shorter now, but it still had that fire he once loved. He wondered if she still used lemon shampoo. His heart beat faster when Grace looked up and glanced in his direction. He couldn't move. *Does she know it's me? No, of course not. Don't lose your nerve now. You've come this far.*

Needing a few minutes to regain his composure, Aidan made a quick turn and headed for the Sports section. He tucked the book he came in with under his arm, grabbed one about football off the shelf and flipped through the pages. Peering over the top of the book, through his sunglasses, he watched her as she talked with fans. He always knew she'd be successful.

Aidan couldn't take his eyes off her. He recalled memories of a pretty young girl standing next to a car on the side of the road. She was still beautiful. He remembered the sound of her laughter and how much in love they were before he ruined everything.

Passages from Grace's book flashed through his mind. When he read Abby's words, Aidan heard Grace's voice pleading with him. He saw the tears running down her face the day he broke both their hearts. It was their story. He was sure of it now. *But, why? Why did she write it? Why did she have Abby find Daniel again? Does she still have feelings for me? Could that be possible? Is there a message in her story?* Aidan only knew he was meant to read her book and that he had to have answers.

She seemed to be wrapping it up. He couldn't let her leave without talking to her. He put the football book back on the shelf. With Grace's novel in his hand, he walked straight to the table, praying she wouldn't have him thrown out.

CHAPTER 12
GRACE AND AIDAN MEET

Grace was thrilled at the turnout. She never knew what to expect at one of these events, especially in a small town. Some women brought books for her to sign. Most purchased their books there. A couple of men showed up out of curiosity. One came to buy *Loving Daniel* for his wife.

"My wife's away on business. A signed copy of your book will make me a hero."

The first hour flew by. Grace enjoyed meeting her readers and talking with them. She liked hearing their comments. *Loving Daniel* seemed to be the favorite of those who had already read it.

"I've read all your books, but this one is my favorite. I had someone like Daniel in my life once and could identify with Abby."

"I brought my copy for you to sign and I'm buying one today as a gift for a friend. I love all your stories, especially this one."

There was a lull around eleven o'clock. Grace checked her messages. Two more from Jonathan. She texted him back to let him know things were going fine, told him she wished he was there and asked about his dad.

The scent of roses coming from behind her made Grace wonder again, who might have sent them. One red rose surrounded by five yellow ones. *If it wasn't Jonathan, then who was it?*

Grace looked up. She noticed a man who had just entered the store. He was wearing jeans and a royal blue shirt with the cuffs rolled up and the top two buttons undone. His jet-black hair, slightly streaked with a few grays, curled over the collar. He looked at least six feet tall and appeared to be about her age. She couldn't see his face that well because of his neatly trimmed beard and sunglasses. The man carried a book in his hand. Grace thought he might be coming to see her. He hesitated then headed for the Sports section. There was something familiar about him she couldn't pinpoint. It made her uncomfortable. He pulled another book off the shelf and thumbed through it. She wondered why he kept the sunglasses on inside the store. Grace thought she caught him looking at her a few times. The strange feeling she had earlier returned. *I'm being silly. Maybe he's just curious about the guest author.*

Grace went back to meeting people and signing books. She forgot about the man with the sunglasses. She glanced at her watch. It was almost noon. Needing to stretch, she stood up.

"Do you have time to sign one more?"

The man from the Sports section was standing in front of her holding out a copy of *Loving Daniel.*

That voice. I know that voice. It couldn't be him...could it? Those hands. Are they the hands that fixed my flat tire all those years ago? No. I'm letting all the talk about Abby and Daniel get to me. I'm imagining things. Why doesn't he take those damn sunglasses off so I can see his eyes?

Her hands trembled slightly, as she took the copy of *Loving Daniel* from him. "Of course. I'd be...happy to. To whom am I signing it?"

He removed the sunglasses and looked straight at her. "Have I changed that much, Gracie?"

Staring into those bluish gray eyes, Grace's knees went weak. *It **is** him. But, why is he here?* She couldn't feel her fingers. The book slipped out of her hands and landed on the table with a loud thud.

"Aidan?"

Watching the color drain from her pretty face, made him feel like a heel. He was afraid she might faint. *I intended to surprise her, not scare the hell out of her.* "I'm sorry. I didn't mean to upset you."

What did he expect? Did he think I'd be overjoyed to see him after all these years? Grace tried to hide what she was feeling. "It's okay. It's just that...well...I didn't expect to see you. What are you doing here?"

He smiled at her. "I wanted an autographed copy of your book."

"You read *Loving Daniel*?"

"I told you someday I'd be reading your books."

Grace was afraid to ask for his opinion. *Has he figured out the story is about us? Is he finally going to tell me what happened?* She sat down. With her hands shaking, she picked up the pen, took a couple of minutes to compose her thoughts and signed the title page.

AMR loves GD 4ever. What happened, Aidan?
Gracie

When she was finished, Grace gave Aidan back his book. He started to open it. "No. Don't read it here. Save it till later."

"If that's what you want."

"It was nice seeing you." Not knowing what else to say to him, she started to pack up.

"Grace, wait. Can we maybe have coffee and talk a bit when you're done here?"

"I...I don't know."

"Please? I can carry stuff to your car. There's a little place across the street. We could have lunch. You must be hungry."

Grace knew there were at least a dozen reasons why she shouldn't go with Aidan. The only thing that came to her mind was the one reason she had to go. *I wanted closure. That's why I wrote the book. Maybe, I'll finally find out why.* Before Grace could answer, Charlene came out of the back room. "Aidan McRae!"

Aidan looked embarrassed. "Hey, Charlene."

Charlene threw her arms around his neck. "It's good to see you. What's with the beard?"

Grace was confused. "You two know each other?"

"Aidan owns a hardware store over in Casselton. Does some carpentry on the side. Built all my shelves. Sounds like you know him too. I hope you take him up on his offer to help. I'm kind of busy right now. Besides, you should never pass up lunch with a handsome man."

Grace wasn't sure how much Charlene overheard, but figured the woman wouldn't stop until she agreed to have lunch with Aidan. Part of her wanted to throw her things in the car and get back to her hotel as fast as she could. However, Grace knew the other part of her, the part that could never refuse Aidan anything, would ultimately win the argument.

"How can I refuse? You tend to your customers, Charlene. Aidan can help me finish up here."

"Great. Come see me before you leave. Good to see you, Aidan. Don't be a stranger."

Grace packed her things into the boxes. Together, they carried them to her car and went back in so she could get the final count from Charlene. "I'll just be a minute."

"I'll get your roses and put them in the car."

Grace spun around to say something, but thought better of it. *How does he know the roses are mine?*

CHAPTER 13
CHARLENE

Charlene moved closer to the window. She watched them walk across the street. *So that's the woman in Aidan McRae's past. The last piece of the puzzle. It wasn't hard to figure out. The strange man who called and asked about Grace Devlin. The roses. Aidan showing up today, unannounced.* She remembered finding one of Grace Madden's books stuck between the cushions on the couch in his living room a few years ago.

"I didn't know you were into romance novels."

He seemed embarrassed, but laughed it off. "Kelli must have left it here."

Charlene had forgotten about it until today when she saw him lurking around the store pretending to read a book with his sunglasses still on. Aidan seemed particularly interested in her guest author.

Wondering what he was up to, Charlene had gone into the back room where she could view his every move on the security monitor. *I was right. He's watching Grace.*

Why is he wearing sunglasses inside and hiding behind a book? It's almost like he's stalking her. I wonder why he doesn't want her to see him.

Charlene stepped out of the back room just as Aidan approached the woman he had obviously come to see. When he took the sunglasses off, there was a look in his eyes she had never seen before. Even his voice was different. He spoke in a soft tone, she had never heard him use.

She continued to observe his peculiar behavior from the doorway and thought about her own relationship with Aidan.

A few months after Charlene opened The Book Nook, she needed work done in the store. A friend recommended Aidan. "He owns a hardware store in Casselton and does carpentry on the side. His work is excellent and he's reasonable."

When Aidan showed up to look at the job she wanted done, he had a little girl with him. "I hope you don't mind that I brought my daughter. She can sit and read a book while we talk. Kelli, this is Mrs. Carter."

Charlene smiled at both of them and spoke directly to the child. "Of course not. Hello, Kelli. It's nice to meet you."

"I like your store."

"Thank you. I'll bet you're about the same age as my son. Mark just turned ten."

"I'm nine."

"Why don't you go over to the children's section while I show your dad what I need done?"

Charlene liked the good-looking carpenter. She wondered if there was a Mrs. McRae. "I haven't been open a year and I'm already in need of more space."

She led him to the back of the store. "I'd like to open this area up more and make room for a small table. I'm hoping you can suggest a way of doing it without knocking down walls. I'm on a tight budget."

He took a small notebook out of his shirt pocket and pulled the measuring tape off his belt. "I'll keep that in mind."

Aidan measured and jotted down numbers as he walked around the store. Charlene hoped he would come up with a solution to her problem she could afford.

"If we rip out this high bookcase shelving in the middle here and get rid of this display rack, it'll give you more space. You'll have plenty of room for a table. I can build shelves on the back wall and in that alcove in the corner. It would be the least expensive way of doing it."

She loved it. "It sounds great. Can you give me an idea of how much it will cost?"

"Let me check on the lumber, Mrs. Carter. I'll get back to you with an estimate in a day or two. Come on Kel. We gotta get home. It's almost time for dinner."

"Please, call me Charlene."

He smiled as he took Kelli's hand and headed toward the door. "Talk to you soon, Charlene."

He worked on Sunday and a couple of nights after the store closed. Her friend was right. Aidan did great work. He was also single.

A week after he finished the job, Aidan stopped in one morning to ask if the shelves were working out okay. Charlene was happy to see him. "How nice of you to follow-up in person. I love the way it came out. Several customers have noticed the changes."

"As long as you're happy."

"I gave your number to a couple of them."

"Thank you. I appreciate it." He rubbed the back of his neck with his hand.

She had the feeling that wasn't the only reason he came. "Is there something else?"

"I was wondering if you'd have dinner with me."

She was delighted. There weren't too many eligible men in town. None like Aidan, anyway. "I'd love to."

On their first date, she found out they had a lot in common. Both were single parents. Their children had both lost one parent. When he found out her husband had been a soldier and was killed in action, Aidan told her about Desert Storm.

They started seeing more of each other. He took her to dinner or an occasional lunch. They took the kids to the movies or bowling. She cooked supper for him and Kelli. He invited them to the lake for barbecues.

Aidan told her he was engaged once. He didn't tell her anything about the woman or why he broke it off. She assumed it was someone from his hometown. He talked more about his failed marriage to Kelli's mother and how he took his daughter to live with him after the woman died.

"I shouldn't have married her in the first place. I didn't love her."

"You were still in love with the one you were engaged to."

He ignored her observation. "Charlene, I care about you a lot. I can talk to you. You understand and you don't judge. You're special to me. I don't want to hurt you. That's why I'm telling you up front, I can't make any commitments."

When they became involved romantically, she thought things had changed. She was wrong. But, it was too late. Charlene was in love with him. Eventually, she realized he wasn't in love with her. *It's not like he didn't warn me.* She wanted more than a one-sided love affair. He understood that.

"You deserve better. I love you as a friend and want you in my life, but I can't give you what you need."

They still went out together and did things with the kids, but only as friends. The romance faded, but their friendship grew stronger. Now, watching the two of them, Charlene knew for sure what she had always suspected. He never got over his first love.

CHAPTER 14
LUNCH AT HATTIE'S

With one arm resting on the flower box, Aidan leaned against the brick wall of the building and thought about the two women inside. *The event seemed like it went well for both of them. I should have let Charlene know I was coming and why. Not that I owe her any explanations, but she's been a good friend. I wonder if she's figured out how I know Grace. Charlene's pretty intuitive and she read the book. I need to apologize for acting like a jerk and putting her in an awkward situation. I'll call her later. Right now, I have a bigger problem. What am I going to talk to Grace about during lunch? Should I just come right out and tell her I know her book's about us and ask her why she wrote it? Probably not a good idea. I wish she'd hurry up. It's hot out here.*

"Sorry to keep you waiting. Charlene wanted to talk about a mutual friend."

"Oh?" *Or should I say oh, oh?*

"J B Blake."

"The guy who writes the crime novels? He's been here a few times. Charlene introduced me to him. Seems like a nice guy."

Relieved he wasn't the "friend" Charlene wanted to discuss, Aidan gave Grace back her car keys and led the way across the street.

Hattie's Place was more spacious than it appeared from outside. The large windows allowed plenty of light to shine through, giving it a bright airy look. The beige walls were decorated with watercolors of quaint little cottages and lake scenes painted by the owner, Hattie Higgins. The tables in the main dining area were close together. At Aidan's request, they were seated at a booth near the back of the room on the bar side.

Aidan spoke first. "Are you hungry?"

"Yes, and I could use a cup of coffee. This is nice. It's larger than I expected."

The waitress came before he had a chance to answer. "Aidan! Haven't seen you in a while. Where you been hiding?"

"Nowhere. Just been busy. Coffee to start. One black and," looking at Grace, "one cream and sugar?"

She was surprised he remembered. "Yes, please."

The woman finally realized he wasn't alone. "Oh my goodness! You're the book lady who was at Charlene's today!"

Grace smiled. "I'm Grace Madden. It's nice to meet you."

Aidan seemed annoyed with the waitress. "I would have introduced you, Trish, if you gave me a chance. Grace, this is Trish Harper."

"I'm sorry. It's just we don't get many celebrities in here. I would have come to the book-signing, but I was working.

Anyway, it's a real pleasure to meet you. I'll leave you two alone to look over the menus. We've got some good specials today. Be right back with those coffees."

"Sorry 'bout that. Trish is a bit over the top sometimes."

"That's okay. I don't mind. Remind me before I head back and I'll leave her a book."

"She'd like that, I'm sure."

"You seem to know everyone. Do you live here?"

"No. I live in Casselton. About a half hour from here. Trish used to live in Casselton. Her daughter and mine are friends."

Grace studied the menu. *He read my book and he drove out of his way to come here.* "Everything looks so good. I'm leaning toward the Chicken Caesar Salad."

"Save room for dessert. Their banana cream pie is the best."

"Better than your mother's?"

"Well…no, but it runs a close second."

Trish brought the coffee. "Would you like a few more minutes?"

Aidan looked at Grace. "I think we know what we want."

Trish took their orders, grabbed the menus and sped off to the kitchen.

Grace stirred her coffee. *This is so awkward. Say something. Ask him about his daughter. Anything.*

Aidan finally broke the silence. "So…did you sell a lot of books?"

"More than I expected to, actually. Charlene was pleased with the event. She wants to do it again."

"That's great. I always knew you'd do well with your writing."

Grace could feel her face turning red. She needed to change the subject. "Enough about me. Tell me about you. How old is your daughter?"

"Kelli's twenty-three."

"My daughter, Elise, just turned twenty-two. Any other children?"

"No. It's been just Kelli and me since she was six. Her mother died in a car accident."

Grace had been wondering if he was married. *If his daughter is about the same age as Elise, he must have gotten married shortly after he left Massachusetts. Not long after he broke up with me.*

"I'm sorry."

"We were divorced when Kelli was two. When Maryann died, I took Kelli."

"You never remarried?"

"No."

"It must have been difficult for you."

"You do what you have to. I've made a lot of mistakes in my life. I wasn't about to add abandoning my daughter to the list."

Grace wondered what other mistakes he was referring to. *Was leaving me one of them?*

"It's not easy raising kids alone," she said.

"I was sorry to hear about your husband. You have a son too, right?"

Aidan seemed to know a lot more about Grace than she realized. "Yes. Jimmy just turned twenty. How did you know about my husband?"

Aidan smiled. "We have newspapers in Maine too. I subscribe to the Globe online. And my dad still lives in Tucker's

Landing. He's friendly with your mom. They've been involved in some community projects and on committees together, I guess."

He stopped talking when Trish returned with their meals. "Can I get you anything else? More coffee?"

Not comfortable discussing Jim, Grace was glad for the interruption and the lull in the conversation. She knew her mother was on some committees with Donald McRae, but Janet seldom talked about him in front of her.

Again, Aidan spoke first. "How's your salad?"

"Very good. How's your sandwich?"

"Great. They use real turkey, not the deli stuff."

Grace tried not to look directly at him. *He used to know what I was thinking. I'm not sure if I like the beard. I wonder why he grew it. His hair looks good longer. I always loved when it got too long and curled at the ends. Other than that and a few gray hairs, it appears he hasn't changed much.*

"So, do I look that different with the beard?"

He can still read my mind.

"Sorry. I didn't mean to put you on the spot. It was just that when you didn't recognize me, I hoped it was the beard and not that I've aged a lot in twenty-four years."

They both laughed.

Her laughter brought him back in time. *I remember the way she laughed at my silly jokes and how she cried at sad movies. She still looks great. How can I get her to see me again?*

She couldn't help but notice the way he was looking at her. *He knows the book is about us. Of course he does.*

"You sent the roses, didn't you Aidan?"

"I didn't like Daniel getting all the glory for my idea."

"They're beautiful. Thank you."

"Now can I ask you something?"

Oh dear. Here it comes. "Okay."

"How well do you know Blake?"

"Jonathan?" Grace breathed a little easier. "He's the one who suggested to Charlene that she invite me here."

She didn't exactly answer my question. Not that she has to. "A business relationship, then?"

What is he trying to find out? "No. Why do you ask?"

Aidan decided he'd better not go there with her just yet. *I better be careful.* "Curious, that's all. Didn't mean to pry. Charlene talks about him a lot. I think she's got a thing for him."

So, he's looking out for Charlene? Why does her love life interest him? "And that bothers you? Are you involved with Charlene?"

Aidan knew he had gone too far. "No. It doesn't bother me. And, no, I'm not involved with Charlene. We're friends and I don't want to see her get hurt."

Grace couldn't believe she asked him that question. "I'm sorry. That's really none of my business. Jonathan was supposed to come with me today. His dad got sick and he had to go to Albany. I thought Charlene seemed disappointed when he couldn't make it. I don't think there's anything going on between them. If there was, I'd know."

"No need to apologize. I shouldn't have brought it up. It's great to see you again, Gracie. How about that pie?"

CHAPTER 15
AFTER LUNCH

It was after two o'clock when they finished lunch. "I'd better be getting back to the hotel. If you walk me to my car, I'll grab that book for Trish."

Aidan was confused. "The hotel? I assumed you were going home from here."

"No. I'm actually taking a well earned mini vacation and spending a few days in the area exploring the antique stores and lovely shops I saw on my way here."

They said good-bye to Trish and left the restaurant. As he walked Grace to her car, Aidan wondered if Blake was originally included in her plans. *She never said they were involved. Of course, she didn't say they weren't either. I can't ask her what I want to know standing on the sidewalk. If I let her go, I'll never find out.*

He waited by the car while Grace dug out a book and wrote something inside. "Please give this to Trish."

"She'll love it. Thanks."

"Thank you for lunch, Aidan. It was great seeing you." *Well that sounded polite and businesslike. I couldn't come up with something better to say to him?*

"So you're not heading home yet?"

"Well…no."

"Have dinner with me tonight. That's if you don't have plans."

Grace hesitated. "I don't think it's a good idea."

"You already have plans for dinner?"

"No, but…"

"What then? You have to eat."

"I was going to have a quiet dinner at the hotel and think about what I want to do over the next few days."

"I can help you with that. I could stop by my store for a while, go home, shower, change and meet you at your hotel around seven. What do you say?"

Grace knew she wanted to see him again. *If there's any chance of ever finding out what I want to know, this is it.* "I never could win an argument with you. Okay. I'm at the Whittier Arms. See you at seven in the lounge."

Aidan closed the car door once she was inside. "I'll be there."

CHAPTER 16
GRACE AT THE HOTEL

Grace carried the roses through the lobby of the Whittier Arms. They were a bit wilted from being in the car. She was glad to get them in the air-conditioned building. "Pretty flowers MS. Madden," said the young blonde desk clerk.

"Thank you. Have a nice afternoon," Grace called to the girl as she headed for the elevator.

Once inside her room, Grace cleared a spot on the desk for the roses. *I knew he sent them. Somehow, I just knew it. He obviously got that I used his idea for Daniel and wanted me to know it. But, why? He didn't seem angry about it.* She closed her eyes and breathed in the sweet scent. It reminded her of the many times Aidan had sent her roses exactly like these when they were young. *We were so much in love. I need to know what happened. Did he come here today to tell me after all these years? Why did he read my book?*

She opened the mini fridge, took out a bottle of water and sat on the chair by the window. Grace let her thoughts drift back to Aidan. There were times during lunch when the conversation was strained and awkward, but there were also moments when it almost seemed like the twenty-four year gap in their relationship didn't exist. They talked about their kids, his business, her career and their college days. *Was he just happy to see an old friend and reminisce about the past, or was there more to it? Is there more to his friendship with Charlene than he's letting on? Why else would he be so interested in Jonathan?*

As she let the cool water quench her thirst, Grace made up her mind. Tonight at dinner, she was going to ask him why he read her book and why he came to the bookstore today.

The ringing of her cell phone interrupted Grace's thoughts.

She fished it out of her bag and saw Jonathan's name. "Hi. How'd it go today?"

"I was just about to call you. It went great. Good turnout. Nice people."

"I got a call from Charlene. She was happy. She'd like to try it again sometime. She's trying to lock in a date to have me do one again on my latest book."

"That's terrific. How's your dad doing?"

"He's hanging in there. They've scheduled the bypass surgery for Friday."

"I hope it goes well. Tell him I'm thinking of him. Keep me posted."

"Thanks. I will. I don't have much time, but I wanted to touch base with you and see how it went. Have you figured out what you're going to do for the next few days?"

"No. I plan to poke around some shops, take some pictures and try the restaurants you suggested."

"Have a good time. Keep in touch. I miss you."

"I miss you too. We'll talk later."

Grace wasn't sure why she neglected to tell Jonathan about Aidan. She hoped Charlene hadn't mentioned it either.

*Come to think of it, Jonathan didn't tell me he had spoken to Charlene until **after** he asked how things went. So, he already knew. That's strange. Maybe there is something more between him and the pretty bookstore owner than he's telling. I think there's more to Aidan's relationship with Charlene than he's divulging too. That would explain his concern. What difference does any of this make to me anyway? Tonight I'll have my answers.*

CHAPTER 17
AIDAN AND CHARLENE

After Aidan dropped Grace's book off to Trish, he decided to stop by and see Charlene. She was behind the counter talking on her cell phone.

"I hope your dad's surgery goes well. We'll talk later. Bye."

Aidan realized she was talking to Blake. "I didn't mean to interrupt anything."

Charlene saw no need to explain she was only leaving a voicemail. "You didn't. How was lunch?"

He ignored the hint of sarcasm in her voice. "Good. Can we talk privately?"

Charlene asked one of the clerks to cover the register and led him into the back room.

Aidan came right to the point. "You know, don't you?"

"That Grace Madden's the woman you've never been able to forget. It wasn't hard to figure out. You come slinking in here, don't bother to look for me and say hello. Then you hide behind your sunglasses and stare at her over a book like some lovesick high school kid. Yeah, I know."

Aidan wished he had handled the whole thing better. "I'm sorry. I should have at least told you I was coming."

"We had dinner together last week. I told you she was coming here and how excited I was about it. You never said a word."

"I know."

"I thought we were friends. It hurts that you didn't trust me enough to tell me."

Aidan felt like a heel. "I never meant to hurt you, Charlene. I hope you know that. You've been a good friend. It's not that I don't trust you. I have trouble talking about my past. You know that. I've told you more than I've ever told anyone."

"Now what? Are you going to see her again?"

"I'm having dinner with her tonight. She's spending a few days in the area. I offered to map out some places she might want to see. She likes antique shops."

"Take her to Portland. I'm sure she'd love it."

"I was thinking that, but I don't know if she'd want to spend the day with me. She could be involved with someone for all I know. She's pretty close to that author friend of yours."

"I think they're just good friends. If it were more than that, she wouldn't have written a book about you. There's a message in her story, Aidan. Go for it. You have nothing to lose."

"What makes you think Grace's book is about me?"

"I had a feeling it was based on a personal experience. A lot of fiction is. When I saw the two of you together, I knew. Women notice things like that."

Aidan gave her a friendly hug. "If you're right, you should take your own advice."

"What do you mean?"

"Men may be slow, but we pick up on things too. You think I don't know you're hung up on Blake? I'll let you know how it goes." With a wink, he turned and walked out of the store.

Aidan decided he wanted to head straight home. He called Sam and asked him to close the store.

"Sure. No problem."

"I'm thinking of taking a few days off if you can handle things alone. I know it's short notice."

"Of course, I can. You could use some time off. Take what you need."

"Thanks. I'll let you know in the morning."

On the drive home, Aidan thought about Grace. *She's even prettier than I remember. What am I doing? Am I following my heart, or chasing a dream? Trying to rekindle an old flame, or relive the past? We're older now. Two different people who no longer have anything in common but their memories.* He thought about what she wrote on the title page of her book. *Then again, maybe Charlene's right. What have I got to lose?*

CHAPTER 18
CHARLENE AND J B

Charlene watched Aidan walk out of the store on the security monitor. *At least he came back to apologize for today and for not confiding in me about Grace.*

I was right. He still has strong feelings for the woman. I hope things work out for him. He deserves to be happy. I wish I knew more about what she's thinking. Why would she want to give a man who broke her heart the chance to do it again, unless she still loves him?

But, what if I'm wrong and Grace and J B are involved? Wouldn't that make a strange love triangle? What are the odds I could have fallen for two guys who are both in love with the same woman? Aidan's right. I need to trust my instincts and follow my own advice. If I don't, I'll always wonder what might have been.

Charlene thought about Jonathan. She was leaving him a voicemail when Aidan walked in and hadn't heard back from him. *I hope his dad's doing okay.*

She was happy to see his number when her cell phone rang. "J B! How are things going with your dad?"

"He's hanging in there. The surgery's scheduled for Friday. I got your message. It was nice of you to call."

"I was thinking of you."

"I talked to Grace. She thought it went well this morning too. She didn't mention the strange caller. Did he ever show up?"

"That was Aidan McRae. Apparently, they're old friends. He took her to lunch."

"Oh?" *Was he the one who sent the roses?* "Did you find out who sent the flowers?"

Charlene wondered why Grace hadn't told Jonathan about Aidan or the roses. Afraid she'd already said too much, she changed the subject.

"They were from a local fan. Speaking of fans, don't forget I want to lock in a date for you to do another author event here at the end of the summer."

"I promise. As soon as I know more on what's happening here."

"Great. I can't wait to see you."

"Really? No reason to wait until the end of the summer to see each other is there?"

Charlene was surprised, but cautious. *Does he mean what I think he does?* "Are you talking business or pleasure?"

Jonathan laughed. "Definitely pleasure. I'd love to come there and take you to dinner when I get back from Albany."

"I'd love it."

CHAPTER 19
DINNER

Aidan was at the bar with a beer in front of him when Grace walked into the restaurant. He stood up and held out a seat for her.

"I thought you might like to have a drink first, but if you're real hungry, we can get a table now."

"This is fine. After that lunch today, I'm not super hungry. I'd love a Pinot Grigio."

Aidan ordered her a glass of wine. "Is this your first visit to Whittier?"

"Yes. It's lovely. The people are so friendly."

"Oh, by the way. Trish said to thank you for the book. You made her day."

Grace picked up her drink. "She's very welcome."

Aidan touched the tip of his bottle to her glass. "To old friends. It's good to see you again, Gracie."

She used to love that he called her Gracie. "You too, Aidan."

After a sufficient amount of small talk, they moved to a table and ordered dinner.

"Have you ever been to Portland?" Aidan asked.

"Once. In fact, I was thinking I might go there tomorrow. They have some great shops and restaurants. I'm sure I can find an antique store or two along the way."

Aidan decided he'd better be careful. He didn't want to appear presumptuous by inviting himself along. "I can help you with that."

"You never liked antiquing."

"No. But, I loved watching you get excited over some old figurine or hundred-year-old postcards from people you didn't know. Just because I don't shop in those places, doesn't mean I don't know where they are. I've lived here a long time. I know the territory."

"How long have you lived here?"

"Long enough to know of a place that sells those funny colored dishes you used to like. The ones you could see through. You still collect 'em?"

She wondered if he deliberately avoided answering her question. "You mean Depression Glass?"

"Yeah, that's the stuff. This guys got all colors, even the dark blue."

"The cobalt blue? Are you serious? I don't collect it anymore, but I kept a few of my favorite pieces and the ones that belonged to my grandmother."

He remembered one piece he bought her. "Still have the blue cup?"

"The Shirley Temple pitcher." She was surprised he remembered that. "I liked it because it had a picture of a little girl on it. I didn't even know who Shirley Temple was. My mother told me when I brought it home. I was doing some cleaning a few years ago and accidentally knocked it off the counter. It broke in a million pieces when it hit the tile floor. I still have the etched glasses."

He had forgotten about the set of green glasses he bought her. "Oh yeah, the ones I got you that day we went to Newburyport. You were going to use them on special occasions."

"And you couldn't understand what was so special about drinking out of someone's old glasses."

They laughed at the memory. She lowered her eyes. "That was such a long time ago."

Neither one spoke for several minutes. Aidan thought about what Charlene said. *She was right. I've got nothing to lose.*

"How would you feel about having some company tomorrow? I could take you into Portland and show you around. I know the best places to eat."

"I don't know, Aidan. That's sweet of you, but…"

"I'm sorry. You're probably involved with someone. I shouldn't have assumed anything."

Grace couldn't blame him. *He must have read my message to him the minute he got outside of the bookstore. I encouraged him further when I agreed to dinner.* "No. It's not that."

"I have another idea. Ogunquit is only about forty-five minutes from here. We could do a few shops on the way and maybe stop in Cape Neddick for lunch. When was the last time you had a hot dog at Flo's?"

Grace smiled, remembering the tiny hot dog stand on the side of the road. "Is that still there?"

"Sure is, but it's not open all day. You have to hit it right."

I don't know why I'm giving him a hard time. I know he's going to talk me into it. Besides, I want to go with him.

"You'll show me the place with all the Depression glass?"

"I'll even call him to make sure he's open."

"Okay, but I'm buying lunch and dinner."

They finished their meal and lingered over coffee. Neither one of them asked the questions they were seeking answers to. Instead, they enjoyed each other's company and reminisced about the past. Both knew they would get their answers when the time was right.

CHAPTER 20
CALL FROM KELLI

It was close to eleven o'clock when Aidan got home. The light was flashing on his answering machine. Before he had a chance to check it, his cell phone rang.

Why is she calling this late? "Kelli. What's wrong?"

"Nothing, Dad. I was going to ask you the same thing. I've been leaving you messages all night."

"I've been out."

"Why weren't you answering your cell? That's not like you."

Aidan knew his daughter worried about him, but he was tired and not in the mood to be grilled. "If you must know, I was on a date."

"Oh, out with Charlene?"

"No."

"Who then?"

"No one you know."

"Oh."

Aidan was losing his patience. "Do you know what time it is?"

"Sorry, Dad."

Feeling guilty for being short with her, Aidan tried to smooth it over. "I'm sorry too, Honey. I ran into an old friend. She's spending a few days in the area. I took her to dinner and offered to show her around tomorrow. It's late and I'm tired. I really need to get some sleep."

"Me too. Have fun tomorrow. Good night."

When he hung up the phone, Aidan shook his head. *Sometimes I wonder which one's the parent.*

CHAPTER 21
ANTIQUITY

Aidan made a short list of antique stores he wanted to show Grace. After a quick breakfast, he showered, shaved and put on a pair of jeans and a light blue polo shirt. When he was ready to leave, Aidan called his friend, Bill Hanley, the owner of Antiquity, the shop with the colored glass. *I hope he didn't decide to go fishing today.*

Aidan was relieved when he answered. "Hey, Bill. Aidan McRae. Are you gonna be open today?"

"In about an hour. You coming by?"

"Yes. Later this morning. I'm bringing a friend. She likes Depression glass. You wouldn't happen to have one of those Shirley Temple pitchers, would you?"

"Yes, I do. It's in mint condition. Want me to put it aside for her?"

"No. I want to buy it and surprise her later. Think you could wrap it in something and hold it for me?"

Bill chuckled at Aidan's request. "You sneaky devil. Leave your truck unlocked. I'll make an excuse to step out for a minute and put it on the floor in the back."

"Great. Thanks, Bill. See you later."

When he arrived at the Whittier Arms at 8:25, Grace was sitting in the lobby. She was dressed casually in a pale green top, white crop pants and sneakers.

Grace stood when she saw him. "Good morning. You're right on time."

She could have just stepped off the page of a magazine. "Good morning," he said. "You look great."

"Thank you."

"I'm glad you're bringing a sweater. It could get cool later."

Once inside his truck, Aidan handed her a piece of paper. "I wrote down a couple of antique stores I know of along the way. If you see someplace else you'd like to stop, tell me. Flo's opens at 11:30. We should try to get there by then. The line starts forming early."

He caught her staring at him. She was smiling. "Something wrong?"

"I like it."

He knew what she meant. "Like what?"

She realized he shaved for her. "Your face. Why'd you get rid of the beard?"

"Oh that. It was beginning to itch."

Aidan always made her laugh. Being with him seemed so natural, yet she had doubts. *What am I doing? Am I trying to relive the past or thinking about the future? Is he? I hope I'm not making a huge mistake.*

She looked at the list. "Which one has the Depression glass?"

"Antiquity. The owner's a friend of mine. We'll go there last, then head for Flo's."

Ten minutes later, they arrived at the first shop. The front lawn was cluttered with flowerpots, wooden signs, lawn statues and an old scrub board. Various sun-catchers and baskets hung from the porch railing. "Bygones. I love the name."

They browsed and noted items that could have belonged to them once. "Hey, I think that's my old fire truck."

Grace laughed. "They say you know you're old when you recognize things in antique stores."

Not finding anything of particular interest, they moved along to the next place on Aidan's list. She bought a few vintage postcards of beaches in Massachusetts.

"We better head to Antiquity now. You'll probably want to spend some time there."

Aidan turned off the main road onto a narrow, winding street. After about a half a mile, he pulled over in front of Antiquity. It was connected to a small house by a breezeway.

"Here we are."

"He has a lot of Depression glass in the window. I can't wait to see what he has inside."

Unlike the other two shops, the entrance to this one was neat and uncluttered. The wicker rocking chair by the door looked like it got a lot of use. "You were right," said Grace as they walked up the pathway to the door. "I would never have found this."

When they stepped inside, a tall, handsome man with graying hair who appeared to be in his late sixties greeted them. "Aidan. Good to see you. I take it this must be your friend who likes Depression glass."

"Nice to see you too, Bill. Yes. This is Grace Madden. Grace, Bill Hanley."

"It's nice to meet you, Mr. Hanley. Your store looks very interesting."

"Madden? The author?"

"Yes," said Aidan. "The author."

"Well, I'll be. My wife reads your books. She's visitin' her sister today in Gorham. Estelle will be so sorry she missed you. Say, if I run over to the house and get the one she's been reading, would you sign it for her?"

"Of course," said Grace.

"Aidan, keep an eye on things, will ya? Ms. Madden, feel free to look around. I'll be right back."

Bill grabbed the package from behind the counter and brought it out to Aidan's truck.

"This place is great. Look at those lamps. And the old typewriter."

Aidan got a kick out of watching her flit around the store like a butterfly not knowing where to land. "Hey, Gracie. Look, cassette tapes. I used to have quite a collection of these and now they're in antique stores. Are we that old?"

Grace laughed. "I remember listening to them in your car."

"We had some great times in that old car."

"Aidan!" She looked around to make sure Bill hadn't come back.

"Sorry."

When Bill returned, he was holding a copy of *Loving Daniel*. "I'll have it over at the register. You can sign it before you leave. Are you looking for anything special or any particular color?"

"Not really, but I love the cobalt blue. You wouldn't have a Shirley Temple pitcher would you?"

Aidan shot him a look. "Had one. Just sold it."

Grace thought about her grandmother, as she looked at all the beautiful colored glass catching the sun through the window. *I'm glad I kept the pieces that were hers and the ones from Aidan.*

"See anything you like?" Aidan asked.

"Oh, yes. I want the blue salt and pepper shakers in the window. They'd look pretty with my dishes. I saw green candleholders and a pretty etched bowl I liked when we came in. I think I'll get those too, if I can find them again."

He followed her to the other side of the store. "Is that them?" Aidan asked, pointing to some green glass on a shelf.

"Yes. Those are the ones."

When she looked closer to check the price, Grace spotted something else.

"Oh, look!"

"Should I see if Bill has shopping carts?"

When she didn't laugh at him, he was afraid he hurt her feelings. She stood staring at the shelf for a minute, not saying a word.

Finally, she turned toward him. "The champagne glasses match the wine goblets."

Aidan reached for one of the glasses. "I'll buy them for you if you promise to use them only on special occasions."

"You don't have to do that."

"I want to. You keep looking around. I'll bring this stuff to the counter and have Bill get the blue things out of the window."

When he finished putting all Grace's treasures by the register, Aidan found her at the back of the store looking at a display of dollhouse furniture. "Some of these pieces are handmade."

"Do you have a dollhouse?

"Yes. It's an old Victorian. I keep it in my office at home. That vanity piece would fit perfectly in one of the bedrooms."

Aidan took it off the shelf and added them to the items at the register.

When Grace finally made her way to the counter, Bill had everything wrapped and ready for her.

"I love your shop. I could spend the whole day here, but I think Aidan's probably getting hungry by now."

"Come back anytime."

Grace paid for her purchases and signed the book for Bill's wife before they left. She promised to return when she could spend more time and Bill said he'd let her know if he came across another Shirley Temple mug.

When they got in the truck, Grace thanked Aidan for everything. "I love that store, Aidan. Bill is so nice. Thank you for taking me there. And, thank you for the glasses. It was sweet of you."

"You're welcome. Now, let's go get some hot dogs."

CHAPTER 22
FLO'S

Cars were parked along both sides of the road when they got to Flo's. Aidan took the first available space he came to.

As they walked past the wooden picnic tables toward the little red building, they could smell the hot dogs. "Well, the line's not outside yet."

Aidan held the rickety screen door open for Grace and saw the customers crammed inside the hole-in-the-wall place. Three people carrying cardboard containers full of hot dogs, chips and sodas were trying to get out.

There were two women behind the counter. One was stuffing hot dogs into rolls. The other was taking orders. "How many dogs?" she'd ask and then write it down on a piece of paper. After taking several orders, she'd cook the hot dogs, let the other woman finish the order and start over again.

Just over six feet tall, Aidan barely cleared the six foot two inch ceiling. "Is it coming back to you?"

"It's like stepping into a time machine. Except for Flo being gone now, it hasn't changed one bit. You said we should get here early."

"No big deal. We're not on a time schedule."

The line moved along. Aidan got two hot dogs with Flo's special relish. Grace ordered one.

When they got outside, a family about to leave offered them seats at their table.

"Timing is everything," he said.

Seated at one of the old picnic tables under a tree, listening to the cars driving by and the screen door creaking, they ate their lunch. Each bite brought back another memory for each of them. They marveled at how sights and sounds and something as simple as eating a hot dog could transport you back in time.

CHAPTER 23
OGUNQUIT

It was one o'clock by the time they got to Ogunquit. Aidan parked in an all-day lot close to Perkins Cove.

"It's a short walk to the center of town. We could browse in some shops, take the trolley back and then have dinner later in Perkins Cove."

Grace wanted to enjoy the warm June day. "Walking off the hot dogs sounds like a good idea."

They walked along Shore Road toward Main Street. She loved the impressive resorts, unique art galleries, restaurants, beautiful homes and the smell of the ocean. "I'd forgotten how pretty it is here."

"Me too. You can get some good shots from the bridge later. Maybe we could venture out onto the Marginal Way if there's time."

"That sounds like fun. Do you come here a lot?"

"No. I used to take Kelli here when she was little. Came with Charlene a few years ago."

Aidan hadn't meant for that to slip out. He knew she'd pick up on it.

"So there **is** more to you and Charlene than friendship."

"Wait." He stopped and turned to face her. "I wasn't totally honest about Charlene and me."

Grace didn't know why it bothered her to hear Aidan had taken someone else to Ogunquit. She pretended to shrug it off. "It's really none of my business."

He took her hand and led her to a small bench. Feeling his strong hand over hers reminded Grace of the way they used to hold hands at the movies. "I don't want secrets between us. Charlene's one of the first people I met when I came here. She lost her husband and was raising a son by herself. We dated for a while. She wanted more out of a relationship than I could give. We remained good friends and go out once in a while. But, it's just as friends."

"I had no idea she's a widow, too."

"She's a good person and deserves to be happy. Between you and me, I was right about Blake. She does have a thing for him."

Grace thought about that for a minute. "I wonder if Jonathan realizes that. He's never said a word."

"Charlene thinks he's hung up on you."

Grace knew she didn't owe him any explanations either, but wanted him to understand her relationship with Jonathan. She pulled her hand from his and turned away before she spoke. "He was for a while, but not anymore. He and my husband were close friends. When Jim died, Jonathan did a lot for me and for my family. We spent a lot of time together.

He helped to get me back on track when I couldn't write for a whole year."

"And fell in love with you?"

"Yes."

Aidan was almost afraid to ask. "And you?"

She turned to face him. "I love him as a friend. Charlene doesn't have to worry about me."

"I'm glad. I wouldn't want to see her hurt."

"Is that why you were so interested in Jonathan?"

"Not entirely." Aidan smiled and stood up. He reached for her hand again. "Let's walk to the beach area. The footbridge is near here."

The beach was less crowded than the center of town. They sat on the wooden benches in the pavilion and watched the waves crash then bubble into a milky, white foam as they crept closer to the sand.

Grace stared out at the Atlantic. She had mixed emotions about being with Aidan. *I should be angry with him, not having fun. What would Jim think? I know he'd want me to be happy.*

Aidan was watching a young couple in the water. They jumped and laughed as each whitecap nearly knocked them over. "It seems like only yesterday we stood barefooted on this beach, ankle deep in the water with our pant legs rolled up. Where did it all go?"

"Maybe we're thinking too much about yesterday, Aidan. That was a long time ago. You can't go backwards in life."

He turned toward her. "No, but you can go forward."

Is he thinking we have a future together? Could that be possible? We're not kids anymore. We have lives and families. "We're not the same people we were back then."

"Then who are we? Things worked out for Abby and Daniel."

"They're fictional characters, Aidan."

He shrugged his shoulders. "Isn't all fiction based on some truth?"

"So, I used a few things from us. Writers do that all the time."

Aidan's tone changed. "I know. Right down to the yellow roses and the gazebo in the rain."

"Why did you read it?"

"I read all your books. Why did you write it?"

Grace didn't know what to say, but she wasn't going to admit anything. "I'm sorry if it bothered you that I used things about us in the book. I never imagined you'd read it and no one else could have known."

He hadn't meant to upset her. *Maybe I was wrong. Maybe that's really all there was to it.* "I'm the one who should be apologizing. It was egotistical of me to think there was a hidden message in it. I had no right to assume anything."

Grace couldn't tell him what she was really upset about had nothing to do with what he said. "It's okay. I can see how you might have thought that."

Aidan knew if there was any chance of a future with Grace he would have to tell her the truth about that day in the gazebo. Sooner or later, he was going to have to tell her. No matter what the outcome, she deserved to know. "The past two days have been the best ones I've had in a long time. It's been great reminiscing, but that's not the only reason."

"That's what upset me," she said. "I've been having a wonderful time, too."

Aidan wasn't sure what she meant. "I don't understand."

"I know I shouldn't, but I feel guilty having such a good time with you."

"Why would you feel guilty?"

"I feel guilty because of Jim."

Aidan searched for the right words to comfort her. "I had no idea you were feeling that way, but I'm glad you told me. I'm sure Jim would have wanted you to go on with your life."

Moving closer, he wrapped one arm around her, gave her a gentle hug and kissed her on the forehead.

He was glad to see the hint of a smile on her face. "Maybe we have been thinking too much about the past. Why don't we concentrate on the present and let the future take care of itself? If we hurry, we can make the next trolley back to Perkins Cove. I think you promised me dinner."

"So I did. But, you're not getting off that easy. I still want to buy a sweatshirt and some salt water taffy."

CHAPTER 24
PERKINS COVE

When they stepped off the trolley in Perkins Cove, Grace could smell the fragrant pink and white sea roses coming from The Marginal Way. As they walked along the narrow street toward the draw-footbridge, she recognized the names of some of the restaurants and boutiques. "I remember Barnacle Billy's and the Oarweed. What was the one we ate at once that had something to do with a storm?"

"The Hurricane. It's been gone for several years. There's another restaurant there now. We could take a look at their menu. I've never been to it, but it's supposed to be good."

From the bridge, they could see all of Perkins Cove. Grace couldn't get enough pictures. "What a gorgeous view!"

"Ever come here with your kids?"

"No. We went to York Beach. They loved the amusement park and the zoo. We stayed at Old Orchard once."

"Old Orchard's nice."

After taking a few selfies of the two of them with the harbor in the background, Aidan took Grace by the hand. "Let's go look for that sweatshirt you wanted."

They browsed through the shops, but didn't buy much. Grace bought a pale blue sweatshirt with a picture of the harbor on it and some saltwater taffy. Aidan got Kelli a tee shirt and a pair of sparkly earrings.

"It's getting late. Why don't we put this stuff in my truck and figure out where we want to have dinner?"

"Good idea."

They decided on Jackie's Too, a popular restaurant in Perkins Cove known for its seafood and ocean views. Since there was a bit of a wait, Aidan made a reservation for six o'clock. "The tide's coming in. We can hang out by the rocks and enjoy the view for a while."

"Great. I can stand on the rocks and take pictures of the waves."

"Not without me hanging on to you."

Grace laughed, but she liked the way he watched out for her. He was the sweet, thoughtful Aidan she remembered.

When they reached a spot that looked flat enough, Aidan stepped up onto the rocks. He held out his hand and pulled her up beside him. "Careful now. I don't want you falling."

"I'll be careful."

It wasn't all that dangerous, but Aidan wasn't taking any chances. He held her tightly by the waist, as she snapped one picture after another.

She felt his breath on her face when he spoke. It sent a shiver through her.

A soft breeze blew her hair against his cheek. "Are you cold?"

"No. I'm fine. It's just so beautiful here."

"Yes. It is a pretty spot."

After a few minutes, Grace turned and faced him. "I think I've got enough. You want to help me down?"

With his hands still around Grace's waist, he pulled her toward him and kissed her. It was a sweet, gentle kiss. Neither said a word. They didn't have to…at least not then.

Aidan led Grace to the edge of the rocks and helped her back down onto the pavement. He fought back the urge to kiss her again. "I think we better go to dinner now."

They held hands as they walked over to the restaurant. Their table was ready. "Follow me," said the hostess. "I have an outside table under the awning for you Ms. Madden. It's right on the water. I'm a big fan of yours."

"Thank you."

Aidan pulled out a chair for Grace. When she sat down, he leaned over her shoulder. "Hanging with a celebrity has some great perks. I like it."

"I'm not a celebrity."

"We've only got the best table in the place. If we were any closer, we'd be IN the water. Look at that view."

Grace looked out at the waves breaking over the rocks. "It's breathtaking."

She picked up her menu. "Remember, dinner's on me. Get whatever you like."

Aidan opened his. "In that case…"

Grace shook her head and laughed. "So, you don't have a problem with a woman buying you dinner? That's good."

"Lunch AND dinner."

She lowered her menu and looked at him. "Two hot dogs at Flo's?"

He leaned forward. Their eyes met. His tone became serious. "I had a great time today."

"Me too, Aidan. The whole day has been wonderful. I can't thank you enough for taking me to the antique stores."

"It was fun watching you get excited over all that old stuff in Bill's store."

"His place is incredible."

Aidan couldn't argue that one. He went back to looking at the menu. "Everything looks so good. What are you going to get?"

"I'm thinking maybe the fried clams. What about you?"

"You talked me into it."

When the waitress came, Grace ordered a glass of white wine.

"I'll have a Bud Light."

Grace liked that he didn't drink a lot and wanted him to know she didn't either. "I enjoy a glass or two of wine with dinner once in a while."

"I've been known to have a couple glasses of wine on occasion, but mostly I drink beer. I stay away from the hard stuff. Plus, I'm driving."

The server brought their drinks and took their orders.

The waves swallowed up the smaller rocks as the tide moved in closer. Seagulls circled over the water. Grace and Aidan, sat quietly for a while, lost in their own private thoughts.

Confused by her erratic emotions, Grace thought about Aidan's kiss. *I shouldn't have let that happen. Is what I'm feeling from the past, or is it how I feel about him now? Why am I getting so carried away? It was just a sweet, simple kiss. That's all. Or, was it?*

Aidan hadn't planned the kiss. It just happened. *I don't think it upset her. She seemed to enjoy it as much as I did. It felt so incredibly good. I'd like to do it again, right here. I wonder what she's thinking. Hope I didn't screw things up.*

Aidan remembered another time in Ogunquit. "How about the day we had lunch at The Hurricane during that storm? We thought the waves would come right through the window."

"I remember all right. We should have been scared to death."

"It was romantic. We were in love. We thought nothing could harm us."

She didn't want to be reminded how much in love they once were. "We were young and stupid and had no business being out in that weather."

"And you call yourself a romance writer."

Grace laughed. He had a point. "I think this is romantic. Dinner at the water's edge. The wonders of nature all around us. Great food. Lots of ambiance. I could use this setting in a novel."

He reached across the table and placed his hand over hers. "What would you call it?"

Interrupted by the server, Grace didn't answer. Aidan let go of her hand. "Food looks great."

Grace ordered a second glass of wine. Aidan had diet soda.

Toward the end of the meal, Aidan asked about her plans for the next day. "What are your plans for tomorrow?"

Grace wasn't sure how to answer his question. "I've been having such a good time, I haven't really thought about tomorrow."

"I don't want to monopolize your whole vacation, but I'd like to see you again, Gracie."

"Maybe I'm the one who's doing the monopolizing. Don't you have a business to run? I've taken you away from your store for two days already."

"I'm the boss. I can take a few days off. I'd like to show you around Casselton a little. My store, where I live, Long Lake. You'd love the lake."

"I don't know, Aidan."

"You don't have to let me know now. Think about it for a while."

Grace didn't know what to do. She liked being with him more than she cared to admit, but another day? *This can't possibly go anywhere, can it? Should it? Do I want it to? Yes, I do need to think about it before I make a big mistake.*

They finished their meal and walked back to his truck. "I'll take the highway and have you back to your hotel by eight-thirty."

Aidan was about to open the door for her when he stopped abruptly. *Oh what the hell.* He wrapped one arm around her waist, turned her toward him and kissed her again.

It wasn't a simple kiss this time. There was no mistaking that.

CHAPTER 25
THE BLUE PITCHER

On the ride back to Whittier, Aidan apologized to Grace for the way he acted in the parking lot. He didn't want her to get the wrong idea. "I don't usually make public displays like that. I'm sorry about what happened back there."

Grace turned her head toward him. "Sorry for the kiss or the public display?"

He kept his eyes on the road. "The display."

Grace wasn't sorry that she kissed him back, either. She thought about both kisses. The first one, on the rocks, was spontaneous and innocent. The second kiss was different. It was the kind she writes about in her books. A burning, passionate kiss that says "I want you." *Nothing innocent about that one. It may have seemed impulsive, but he put some thought into that kiss.*

"You've been reading too many romance novels," she said, jokingly.

"Ya think?"

They didn't talk much the rest of the way back. Both were content listening to soft music on the radio. Grace fell asleep before they got back into Whittier.

When they arrived at the hotel, Aidan pulled into a parking space. He turned toward Grace and gave her a gentle nudge. "Wake up sleepyhead."

She was a little disoriented at first. "Where are we?"

"Your hotel. You nodded off a few miles back."

"I'm sorry. It must have been the wine."

He pushed a few strands of hair away from her face. "That's okay. As long as it wasn't the company."

She shifted her body to face him. "Thank you for today, Aidan. I had a wonderful time. I loved Bill's shop. It was sweet of you to buy me the champagne glasses."

"Well, they do match the others and you need them for special occasions."

Grace laughed. "Like you know one glass from another."

"You got me there. Do you think we have time for a cup of coffee before I head home? I could use one about now."

"Yes, of course. You must be tired too." She reached for the door handle. "My car's over there. Why don't we put my stuff in the trunk and then go inside for coffee?"

"Wait. Before we do that, I've got something else for you."

"Something else?"

"Just sit tight a minute. I have to get it out of the back."

Grace wondered what he was up to.

When he got back inside the truck, Aidan handed her a plastic bag. "I didn't have time to wrap it fancy."

Grace looked in the bag and saw a box wrapped in brown paper like the kind Bill had used to wrap her items. "What's this?"

"Open it."

She pulled the box out and tore at the wrapping. "You didn't have to get me anything else."

"I wanted to."

When she opened the box and saw the blue glass, her face lit up. "The Shirley Temple pitcher. But, Bill said he sold his last one."

"He did. He sold it to me this morning over the phone. I asked him to put it aside."

Grace took the pitcher out, held it by the handle and thought about the first one he had given her. She treasured it for years because it reminded her of Aidan and the day they spent in Newburyport so many years ago. When she accidentally broke the mug, it upset her terribly. She could have found a replacement online, but it wouldn't have meant as much.

"It's beautiful," she said, swiping at a tear. "I'll try not to break this one. I won't even wash it."

She tucked the small pitcher safely back in the box, placed it between them on the seat and moved closer to him. "Thank you, Aidan."

Grace threw her arms around his neck and gave him a long, smoldering kiss that suggested more than gratitude. When she started to pull away, Aidan slipped one arm around her shoulder and pulled her closer. He liked the way she nestled up against him. "Don't worry about breaking it. It's only a cup."

"It's more than that."

I know, he thought. *Much more.* "Have you decided about tomorrow yet?"

Grace was nervous about where this might be heading, but she couldn't seem to help herself. *We've been together for most of the last two days. So far, he's carefully avoided answering my questions. How can I even think about a relationship with him after what he did to me? Would I ever be able to trust this man again? On the other hand, I haven't exactly been up front with him about Loving Daniel.*

I only know I don't want to spend the rest of my life wondering what might have been. I've done enough of that. "I'd love to see where you live."

Aidan knew if he kissed her again, it would be too difficult to stop. Not wanting to spend the rest of the night in his truck, he lightly brushed his lips to her forehead and removed his arm.

"It's getting late. Why don't we get that coffee and I'll tell you how to get to my house?"

CHAPTER 26
JONATHAN'S PHONE CALL

Grace kicked off her shoes and dropped her purse on the desk. It was almost ten o'clock. The bed looked inviting, but she was too keyed up to sleep. She took the blue pitcher out of the box, sat in the wing-backed chair and thought about Aidan.

He's thoughtful, sensitive and funny. He could have told Bill to hold the pitcher for me, but he knew it would mean more if it came from him. Is the Aidan I've spent the past two days with the one I fell in love with? Or, is he the Aidan who broke my heart?

The ding of her cell phone startled Grace. She got up, put the mug on the desk and checked her messages. It was Jonathan. She'd forgotten all about him.

Are you still awake?

Yes. How's it going?

Can I call you? I need to talk.

Grace felt guilty she hadn't called him today to ask about his dad.

Yes.

"Hi. I know it's late. This is the first chance I've had to call. It's been a tough day."

He sounded down. "You can call me anytime. What's happening? How's your dad?"

"He was fine yesterday. This morning his cardiologist ran more tests. They decided to move the surgery up to tomorrow. It scared my mother. It took a while to convince her it was a good idea."

"Oh dear. How's he with moving it up?"

"He's okay. I think he just wants to get it over with. My mom's trying to put on a brave front, but it's taking a toll on her."

"I'm sure she's glad you're there."

Jonathan wanted to hear about her trip. "So, how's the vacation going?"

"Great. Plenty of good restaurants. I love the shops and antique stores."

"Doing a lot of shopping?"

"Some."

"You've had good weather."

"Yes, the weather's been perfect."

He had the feeling she didn't want to talk about her trip. "I'm glad you're having a good time. You needed a vacation. Still coming home Friday?"

"Yes. I'll be heading home Friday morning. I might make a few stops along the way."

"Well, it's getting late. I'll let you get some rest."

"You too. I hope everything goes well tomorrow. I'll say a prayer for all of you. Let me know as soon as you can. Call me if you need me."

"Thanks, I will. Good night."

Grace wasn't sure why she still didn't tell Jonathan about Aidan. *I just don't think he'd understand and I'm too tired to explain it tonight. It's not like I lied to him. Okay, so a lie of omission is a lie. He's got enough on his mind right now. He doesn't need to worry about me. Besides, I might never see Aidan again after tomorrow.*

Not wanting to think about that possibility, Grace brushed her teeth and changed into her pajamas. With the blue mug where she could see it, she set the alarm on her phone and got into bed.

Grace was almost asleep when she heard the ding of her phone again. Thinking it was Jonathan, her first thought was to ignore it. *I'd better not. It could be one of the kids.*

Nite Gracie.

Good night Aidan.

Smiling, she closed her eyes and went to sleep.

CHAPTER 27
CHARLENE'S MESSAGE

Jonathan wondered why Grace had been so vague about the past two days. *It's obvious she doesn't want me to know about her lunch with Aidan McRae. But, why? So what if she had lunch with an old friend? Maybe she was tired and didn't want to get into it.*

He began to feel guilty. *I left out stuff too. I didn't tell Grace I knew about her lunch date with Aidan and I figured out he sent the roses. Charlene didn't mean to cause trouble. I pumped her for information and led her to think I already knew."*

Jonathan decided he had more important things to worry about. *Grace is an adult. She's capable of taking care of herself. If she wanted my advice, she'd ask for it. Right now, my family needs me. I have to concentrate on them.*

He was just about to plug his phone into the charger when it buzzed.

Wanted to let you know I'm thinking of you. Keep positive thoughts. Everything's going to be fine. Call me if you need to talk.

Thank you, Charlene. I'll call you tomorrow. Nite.

Charlene really is a sweet person. I wonder why it took me so long to realize it.

CHAPTER 28
GRACE IN CASSELTON

It was a little after nine o'clock on Thursday morning, the last day of her vacation, when Grace arrived at Aidan's. With her fingers wrapped tightly around the steering wheel, she pulled in and parked behind his truck. *I hope coming here wasn't a mistake.*

Aidan was in the front yard. The smile on his face as he walked toward her car erased any doubts she had. Grace let go of the wheel and stepped out onto the unpaved driveway. Sunlight streamed through the tall pine trees.

He gave her a quick kiss on the cheek. "I'm glad to see you found it okay. Coffee's all made. I'm sure you could use some after the long drive."

"Coffee sounds good."

He led her along the brick path to the mustard yellow, two-story house. "This is nice. It's so quiet here. You have a lot of land."

"Wait till you see the back."

When they got to the huge covered porch, he stopped and pointed to the flower baskets hanging from the white beams. "I'm not much of a gardener. Those red geraniums and a few planters out back are about all I can handle."

"This looks like something out of a magazine. The wicker chairs remind me of how people used to sit on their verandas and have lemonade on a hot summer day."

"Thanks. I did the porch myself."

She followed him into the living room. The pine walls and dark wood beams gave it a rustic look. "The house is larger than it appears from the outside. I love the fieldstone fireplace."

She could see him stretched out on the chestnut brown sectional sofa watching tv, or sitting in the matching recliner reading the paper.

"Did you do the kitchen? The countertops look new."

"I did them a few years ago and bought new appliances. Those are the original cabinets."

Aidan took a carton of milk out of the fridge. He filled two mugs with coffee, added the milk and sugar to one and handed it to Grace. Let's go out on the deck. I'll show you the rest of the house later."

They stepped out onto the huge deck that ran almost the width of the house and extended out at least ten feet. Pots of flowers were on either side of the stairs leading to the grassy area below. "You weren't kidding about the back of the house."

Grace stood at the railing and looked out at Long Lake. "It's beautiful here. So quiet and serene. That's Paradise to a writer."

"It's not always this quiet, but it is beautiful. You're welcome to come here to write anytime."

Grace could feel her cheeks turning red. "You've got such an incredible view. You can see clear across the lake."

"I had to build the deck up high because of the way the land slopes down to the lake."

"You built the deck too?"

"It gave us more living space in the summer months. I like to barbecue and it came in handy when Kelli had friends over."

He brought her to the glass umbrella table. "Let's sit and have our coffee. Then we'll go down by the water."

"Do you have a boat?"

"No. Maybe someday, but right now, I don't have the time or money for expensive hobbies like boating."

"Sometimes, someday never comes. That's what Jim used to say."

Aidan sensed sadness in her voice. "I was thinking, since we did so much yesterday, we should slow the pace down today. I'd like to show you my store. Then I thought we'd come back here for lunch and a swim. I can throw something on the grill for dinner or we can go out. Did you bring a bathing suit?"

Grace sat back and enjoyed the view. "Yes, I did. A relaxing day sounds wonderful and I'd love to see your store."

It was a short walk to the edge of the lake. "Sometimes I sit down here and read, or just think."

Grace pictured him sitting in one of the white Adirondack chairs by the water reading *Loving Daniel*. She wondered what he thought about when he sat alone in this peaceful, private place.

Aidan turned to face her. The sunlight made her eyes a deeper shade of green. He thought about last night and how soft her lips felt on his. Slipping his arms around her waist, he kissed her gently. Did he detect the scent of lemon in her hair or only imagine it? He held her tightly for several minutes after the kiss, before reluctantly pulling away. "Why don't we take that ride into town now?"

"Do I get the grand tour first?"

"You saw most of the downstairs when you came in."

"There's more?"

"Just my office."

Once back inside, he showed her a small room off the main living area. "This was originally the third bedroom. I use it for an office. It was bigger, but I put a half bathroom in here."

"You've done a lot of work."

"It was a camp when I bought it. I winterized it and turned it into a year round home for Kelli and me. The living area was pretty much what you see now, except for the hardwood floors. Adding the sliders let in a lot more light. Eventually, I built the deck."

He took her upstairs. "Except for the floors and updating the bathroom, I haven't done a lot up here other than paint. The master bedroom is small. I've thought about taking out the wall and making one big bedroom, but Kelli stays over once in a while and my dad comes to visit on occasion. I don't really need a bigger room."

When they got back downstairs, Aidan grabbed his car keys off the counter. It's almost eleven. Ready to take a ride?"

"Ready when you are."

It only took a few minutes to get to town. Aidan pointed to a building on the right. Grace saw the sign. McRae Hardware.

"That's my store. I'll show you the rest of the area first. We'll come back here."

Aidan showed her the town hall, public library and a few other interesting places. He pulled over near what looked like a park. "Let's get out and walk a little."

"This is pretty. What is it?"

"Crystal Lake Park. I want to show you something."

Grace walked along side of him, stopping short when she saw it. " A gazebo," she said, barely above a whisper.

"Just for a minute. Please. I want you to see the view from here."

They walked up the stone path to the wooden structure that was a much larger version of the one in Grace's back yard. The one they used to sit in and talk about their future. As they stood inside looking out at the lake, images of them in the gazebo back home flashed through her mind.

"Why?"

"It reminds me of home."

"Do you ever get homesick, Aidan?"

"Sometimes. When I do, I come here."

She remembered how hard it was raining the day he broke up with her in the gazebo at home. Does he think of that when he comes here? All she could say was, "It's lovely."

Aidan realized bringing her there was a mistake. "I didn't mean to upset you. We can leave now. I'll show you the store and then we'll have a relaxing afternoon at the lake. I promise."

After introducing Grace to Sam and another employee, Aidan showed her around.

"It's an interesting store. No wonder you're so proud of it."

As they were leaving, Sam gave him a wink. "You come back and see us again."

CHAPTER 29
KELLI

Aidan shouldn't have promised a relaxing afternoon when he knew they both still had questions that needed answers. He had to know why she wrote the book. If he let her leave without telling her the truth about that day in the gazebo, Aidan knew he might never see Grace again.

They were both quiet the rest of the way back to his house. When he pulled into the driveway, there was a red SUV behind Grace's car. "Looks like you have company."

He looked concerned. "That's my daughter's car. I wonder what she's doing here."

When they entered the house, Kelli was in the kitchen. "Hi, Dad."

"Kelli. What are doing here? Is everything okay?"

"Of course. I needed some important papers I left in my room. I was just about to leave when I heard you pull up."

"Why didn't you call?"

"I didn't know I had to."

Loving Daniel

Aidan felt foolish for acting so defensive. "Of course, you don't have to. I just got a little nervous seeing you here this time of day. I thought something was wrong."

She seemed annoyed. "Ah, Dad."

"What?"

"Do you think you could introduce me?"

"Oh, Honey, I'm sorry. Kelli, this is Grace Madden. She's an old friend from back home."

"Grace, this is my daughter, Kelli."

Grace figured the girl got her height from Aidan, but the strawberry blonde hair had to be from her mother. "It's a pleasure to meet you, Kelli. Your dad's told me a lot about you."

"It's nice to meet you, too. Dad doesn't talk much about people he knew in Massachusetts. Wait a minute. Madden? Are you the author who was at the bookstore in Whittier the other day?"

Aidan answered for her. "Yes, she's the one. I've been showing her around town. Gracie and I were about to have some lunch and go for a swim. Have you eaten? You're welcome to join us."

Gracie? Kelli knew when three's a crowd. "No thanks, Dad. I already helped myself and I do have to get back to work. Again, it was nice to meet you, Ms. Madden."

"Call me Grace. Please."

"Goody-bye, Grace. Hope to see you again. I'd love to hear stories about my dad."

Kelli gave Aidan a kiss on the cheek and a hug. "At least now I know why you've been reading romance novels. I was beginning to worry."

CHAPTER 30
THE SWIM

Aidan was glad Kelli didn't stay for lunch. He wanted to be alone with Grace. Having his daughter there would have made him self-conscious. "It's getting hot out. How about a sandwich? Then we can relax for a while before that swim. I have tuna or chicken salad, Rye bread, pickles, and lemonade, water or diet soda."

"Chicken sounds good and lemonade."

Grace carried the pitcher of lemonade and two glasses out to the deck while Aidan made the sandwiches. She checked her phone. A text from Elise and a voicemail from Valerie. Both asked if she's having a good time. Nothing from Jonathan yet. She shot him a quick text.

Thinking of you. Hope everything's OK.

Just as Aidan came out, Jonathan texted her back.

Thanks. Can't talk now. He's in recovery.

"One of your kids?"

"No. Jonathan. They moved his dad's surgery up to today."

"I hadn't realized. Is he okay?"

"He's in recovery. He'll let me know later."

After lunch, they changed into their swimsuits, put sunscreen on, grabbed towels and went down by the water. They sat in the Adirondack chairs looking out at the lake.

"Your daughter is very pretty. She has your eyes. I hope my presence didn't make her feel uncomfortable."

"Thanks. I'm sure it didn't bother her. Kelli tends to be overprotective of me, but she knows I date once in a while. She was probably caught off guard because I don't usually bring anyone here."

"You've been the only parent she's known for most of her life. Can't blame her."

"Yeah, but it reminded me of when my mother found my Playboy magazines under my mattress."

They both got a good laugh out of it.

"This is such a lovely place. I could sit here with my laptop and write all day."

"What would you write about?"

"Oh, I don't know. Two people stranded on an island when their rowboat floats away while they're making love on the beach."

"I think that's been done."

"Something would come to me, I'm sure."

"It's hot. Let's go for that swim."

The water was cold. Grace shrieked and tried to go back. Aidan grabbed her hand and pulled her in further. "Oh, no you don't. We're in this together."

"But, it's cold!"

"Wimp. You're only in up to your knees."

"I'm not a wimp."

"Prove it."

Grace dropped her other hand in the water and splashed him. When the icy water hit his bare chest, Aidan let out a yell.

"Now who's a wimp?"

He let go of her hand, went out to his waist and ducked all the way in. She laughed at the way he shook his head back and forth when he came up.

"You look like a wet dog."

Before she could run, he was right there. "Aidan, no! It's too cold!" He grabbed both arms this time and pulled her in up to her waist.

"Not once you get used to it."

Knowing he was going to throw her in, she beat him to it and went under. "Are you happy now?"

Side by side, they swam further out. Aidan was a strong swimmer, but Grace kept up with him. They floated near the end of the pier for a while. "This is about as far out as we should go. It gets pretty deep past here."

"It's been a long time since I've gone swimming in a lake. It seems weird not to have waves coming at you."

"You kept up pretty good. Do you still go to the beach a lot?"

"Not as much as I'd like to. We have a pool."

They swam back to where the water was shallow enough for them to stand up. It was up to Grace's chest. She felt the warmth of the afternoon sun on her shoulders. Aidan brushed a few matted strands of hair away from her cheeks. Taking her face in his hands, he leaned forward and kissed her.

Grace closed her eyes when their lips touched. His kiss was gentle. He smelled of sunscreen. She held onto his strong arms. There was no doubt her feelings were about now, not the past. *What am I going to do? How could this possibly work?*

Aidan dropped his arms down around her waist and pulled her closer. He kissed her shoulders and worked his way back up to her lips. She reached up and slid her arms around his neck. The feel of her soft wet skin awakened all his senses. Even in the cold water, Grace could tell how much he wanted her. She pulled back a little and looked up at him.

"Why did you go to the bookstore Tuesday?"

"To see you."

"What do you think about when you sit alone by the water?"

His expression turned serious.

"The past. Sometimes I think about you and what might have been if I hadn't messed it up. Have you ever thought about me over the years?"

She looked away. "Yes."

He took her chin in his hand and gently turned her face toward him again. "Am I Daniel?"

Tears welled in her eyes. "Abby and Daniel were supposed to be fictitious characters. No one was supposed to know. I never thought you'd read it."

"Why did you write it, Gracie?"

"I don't know. I'm a romance writer. I found my old diary and some letters you sent me up in the attic. I started reading them. I thought it would make a good story."

"You saved my letters?"

Grace wished she hadn't started this conversation. Shivering, she freed herself from his grip.

"Your lips are turning blue. We need to get you dry."

He lifted her out of the water and carried her back to the chairs. With pine needles caught between her toes, she stood dripping and shaking. Aidan quickly grabbed a beach towel, dried her off and draped it around her. He used another towel for her hair before drying himself.

"Feel warmer?"

Her teeth were still chattering. "Maybe we should go back to the house so you can change into some dry clothes."

"Yes. It's getting late anyway."

When they got in the house, Aidan brought her upstairs. "Why don't you take a nice hot shower? I'll throw something on the grill later."

She wasn't sure about staying for dinner, but the shower sounded great. "A shower sounds good."

"There's fresh towels on the rack and a clean robe on the back of the door you can put over you."

Grace stepped into the tub. As the hot, steamy water warmed her, she thought of what Aidan said earlier. *Maybe the past doesn't matter anymore. We've both wasted too much precious time on the past and regrets. Now is what's important. Haven't I learned anything these past few years?*

CHAPTER 31
AT THE LAKE

Grace felt much better after she showered and dried her hair. With Aidan's robe around her, she walked into his bedroom to get dressed.

"Aidan! I didn't know you were in here." Instinctively, she pulled the robe tighter.

He was standing by the chest of drawers wearing only a pair of black cargo shorts. "Sorry if I startled you. I came in to get a clean shirt."

"It's okay. I just didn't expect to see you."

"Nice robe," he said, thinking how sexy she looked.

"You like it?"

Happy to see her smiling again, he walked toward her. "Looks better on you than it does on me."

"You think so?"

"Oh, yeah," Aidan said, as he hugged her and kissed the top of her head. "I'm sorry Grace. I promised you a relaxing day."

"It's not all your fault. I'm partly to blame. Both of us have been avoiding things we know we have to talk to about."

"You're right."

She looked up at him. "Maybe we should stop wasting our time on the past. Does it really matter now?"

"Yes. I don't want it hanging over us for the rest of our lives. You'd always wonder. I owe you an explanation."

He brought her over by the bed and sat down next to her.

"Breaking up with you that day in the gazebo was the hardest thing I've ever done. I've regretted it to this day."

"You never gave me a reason. When I re-read your letters, even all these years later, I still wondered what I did that made you stop loving me. I thought if I wrote about us, it would give me some kind of closure."

"I've never stopped loving you."

Grace hadn't expected that. "Then why did you leave me?"

"When I came home after Desert Storm, I was confused about things. Things I couldn't talk about. Not to anyone. Even you. Especially not you."

"I would have understood whatever it was. What I couldn't understand was your not giving me a reason."

"When I was injured, I spent a lot of time in a hospital before I came home."

"You didn't want to talk about it. I begged you to talk about it. I would have listened."

"I couldn't. I couldn't talk about the things I'd seen and done. I couldn't explain what I was going through to anyone. The nightmares, the anxiety, freaking out when I heard a loud noise, fear of being in a crowd. Emotional scars never heal. I didn't want to put you through that."

"Maybe I could have helped."

Aidan looked straight at her and finally told her what she needed to know. "Gracie, they told me in the hospital I had permanent nerve damage and might never be able to have children."

He waited for her reaction, wondering how she'd take it.

It only took her a minute to process what he said. Her eyes clouded. She reached up and stroked his face. "Oh, Aidan. I loved you. It wouldn't have mattered."

"I know. That's why I couldn't tell you. I was afraid I couldn't give you the kind of life you deserved and I knew you'd have stayed with me anyway. I didn't want you to stay with me out of pity or end up resenting me."

"I wouldn't have stayed with you out of pity. You should have had more faith in me."

"But, I didn't. I was young and confused. I'd been through things I was sure only someone who'd been in combat could understand."

Grace thought about Kelli. "But, you have a daughter?"

"I met Maryann shortly after I moved to Maine. We went out a few times. One night she invited me to a party at her house. I was drinking. She didn't think I should drive and said I could spend the night. Well, one thing led to another. When she told me she was pregnant, I didn't believe I was the father. Even after I explained why, Maryann insisted it was my child. A paternity test confirmed it."

"So you married her?"

"It was too late to go back home. You were married to Jim by then. I couldn't leave her and my unborn child. I wanted to do what was right, but I made Maryann's life miserable. We divorced after two years."

She placed both hands on his shoulders and looked up at him. "But, you owned up to your responsibility after she died. A lot of men wouldn't have done that. It's not easy being a single parent. You made a life for yourself and Kelli. A good one."

"You've had a good life, haven't you Gracie?"

Her eyes filled with tears. She finally had her answer. She could forgive him now. "Yes, Aidan. I had a good life with Jim. I have two great kids and a successful career. You can let go of the guilt now."

Grace let her hands slide down to his chest. She liked touching him and hearing his heartbeat quicken when she brushed her lips over his bare skin.

Taking her face in his hands, he wiped the tears from her cheeks with his thumbs. "Don't cry, Gracie. Everything's gonna be okay."

At that moment, she believed him. *It's time for me to let go of some things too and start to live again.*

The robe slipped a little on one side. Aidan kissed the exposed shoulder and worked his way up to her lips. He kissed her long and hard. It tortured him knowing she had nothing underneath. He wanted to feel the softness of her skin, not terrycloth. Slowly, he slid it down to her elbows. She shook her arms from the sleeves. Taking her by the hands, he pulled her up off the bed, letting the robe fall to the floor.

Aidan wanted to make love to Grace since the night he fell asleep reading her book and dreamed of her. Like in the dream, he pictured her coppery hair fanned across his pillow and felt the heat from her body. Only now, she was standing in front of him. Her image wouldn't fade when he touched her. His fantasy was about to become a reality.

Pulling her close to him, Aidan rubbed her back and kissed her neck. His hands slid over her smooth skin. She smelled of lavender. He lifted her onto the bed, undressed and got in beside her. Wrapping her arms around his chest, she snuggled against him. Her body was warm, yet he felt her shiver again.

"Are you cold?"

Grace smiled. "Not at all."

This time, it wasn't the cold water from the lake that made her shiver.

CHAPTER 32
AFTER THE LOVING

Grace was awake when Aidan finished his shower and went back into the bedroom. "How long was I sleeping?"
"About a half hour."
"What time is it?"
"Five-thirty. Are you hungry?"
"I'm starving."
"I'll go downstairs and get things started. Shower's all yours again. Come down when you're ready."
Grace thought about Aidan as she let the hot water rinse off the soap. She hadn't meant to let things go that far. Or, had she? Kissing in his truck last night brought back a lot of memories. This afternoon, when they were in the lake, she found herself wondering what it would be like to be with him again after all these years. Would it be the same? Would they feel awkward with each other? Were they both chasing dreams and living in the past?
When she got out of the shower, Grace went back into the bedroom to get dressed. The sight of the rumpled sheets

made her smile. Making love with Aidan was so different now than when they were in college. She wasn't a shy, inexperienced young woman in love for the first time. He wasn't an eager young man in a hurry. Aidan was confident, gentle and unselfish. There was a passion in their lovemaking Grace had never known before. *No, we're not chasing dreams or living in the past. Our feelings are as real now as they ever were. But, where do we go from here?*

Aidan was taking steaks out of the fridge when Grace got downstairs. The table in the dining area was set with plain white plates on red placemats. A candle flickered in the center of the lazy Susan.

"Everything looks lovely. What can I do to help?"

"You could make the salad. Stuff's on the counter. I'll throw these on the grill."

Aidan walked past her, as she headed for the kitchen. With both hands holding the plate, he leaned in and kissed Grace on the cheek. "You were incredible. I'll be right back."

Too embarrassed to answer, she started washing the lettuce. He called to her from the deck. "There's potato salad in the fridge. Bread's on the counter. I have wine, if you want it. How do you like your steak?"

"Medium rare please. Diet soda for me. I have to drive back to the hotel later."

Aidan was glad she couldn't see his disappointment. He was hoping she'd spend the night. *Maybe after supper, I can talk her into it.*

After dinner, they cleaned up the kitchen, started the dishwasher and walked down to the water. The big orange ball, its glow skimming the lake, looked as if it had been painted on the darkening sky before it disappeared into the horizon.

"What a gorgeous sunset. I'd like to use it in a story sometime."

Aidan slipped his arm around her waist, hugged her and laughed. "Writers."

"Thank you for the great dinner and the lovely sunset. It's been a wonderful day, but it's getting late. I'd better get going."

"Do you really have to leave?"

"What?"

"Why not stay here tonight instead of driving back to Whittier?"

"For one thing, I have to pack. I'm checking out in the morning."

"Do you have to go home tomorrow?"

"Yes, Aidan. I do."

"Sure I couldn't talk you into one more day?"

"How would I explain where I am to my kids? How would you explain me to Kelli, if she came back?"

She had a point, but he was afraid to let her go. "I hadn't thought of that. I just want us to be together as much as possible. When will I see you again?"

As much as Grace wanted that too, she still wasn't totally convinced a relationship with Aidan was possible. He seemed to think they could pick up where they left off before he went away. It wasn't that easy. She needed time to think and couldn't do that here.

"I don't know."

"But, you do want to see me again, don't you?"

"Of course I do, but it's not that easy."

He didn't understand her reasoning. *Why is she creating roadblocks?* "It is if we don't make it difficult."

"I'm not trying to make it difficult, Aidan, but we need to think about what we're doing."

"I've done all my thinking."

"Well, I haven't. I need time. You seem to think we can pick up where we left off more than two decades ago and live happily ever after. We're not college kids anymore. We're adults with responsibilities and families to consider. Our lifestyles are different. We live miles apart."

"I know all that, but we can work it out."

"You don't know that for sure."

"Life doesn't come with guarantees. The only thing I'm sure of is our someday is here and we can't let it get away from us this time."

"Maybe you're right, but I still have to go home. I have things to do and people coming over on the weekend and I have to call Jonathan. His dad was just coming out of surgery the last I heard and he couldn't talk right then."

"Okay. You win. Oh. I got a text from Charlene while you were in the shower. He's out of recovery. Sorry, I forgot to tell you."

Grace was surprised that Jonathan contacted Charlene and not her. "Thanks."

Aidan carried Grace's bag to her car. "Text me when you get to your hotel so I'll know you got back okay."

"I will. Goodnight. Thanks again for everything."

Not knowing when he'd see her again, Aidan gave Grace a long, lingering kiss before opening the door. He wanted to leave her with a positive thought. "While you're mulling things over, remember I meant what I said. I never stopped loving you."

CHAPTER 33
CALL FROM JONATHAN

Grace sent Aidan a text when she got back in her hotel room.

Safely in my room. Need to pack. Then to bed. Good night.

Have a safe trip. Let me know when you get home. Nite Gracie.

Yawning, she pulled her suitcase out of the closet. *It's been a long day. I better text Jonathan while I pack.*

Before she had a chance to type in a message, her phone rang.

"Jonathan. Hi. I was just about to text you. How's your dad doing?"

"He's doing very well. If he continues to improve over the weekend and is out of ICU, I plan to head home Monday or Tuesday."

"What about your mom?"

"She's doing fine. My sister will be around. I have an important meeting in Boston Wednesday with my publisher. I'd like to make it if I can. Of course, it all hinges on my dad. What about you? Still going home tomorrow?"

"Yes. Check-out's eleven, but I'd like to be on the road earlier."

"Listen, if everything goes as planned and I'm home Wednesday, how 'bout lunch on Thursday? We can catch up."

"That would be nice. I'll hold it open. You can let me know for sure later."

"Great. I'll be in touch. I've missed you."

"I've missed you too. I need to pack and get some sleep. Talk to you soon."

"Good night Grace."

Grace wondered why Jonathan didn't ask any questions about what she did today. *I wonder if he knows about Aidan. He's been in contact with Charlene and she sent Aidan a text. If she knows, it's a pretty good bet, he knows. I'm going to have to tell him anyway, but I wanted it to come from me. Maybe Aidan's right and there is something developing between Jonathan and Charlene. It should be an interesting lunch.*

CHAPTER 34
AIDAN ALONE AGAIN

Friday morning, Aidan had his coffee down by the water. He enjoyed the serenity of the lake before the boaters were out. He wished he could have convinced Grace to stay one more day, but understood why she had to leave. *She's right. There's a lot to consider. How can I expect to pick up a relationship with a twenty-four year gap?*

In his head, he knew that. In his heart, he was worried. What she said made sense. Sitting in one of the Adirondack chairs, he thought about Grace and the events of the past few days. *By now, she's on her way home. What's gonna happen when she's back with her family and friends? Will she tell them about me? How? She can't sit down at the dinner table and casually mention she spent the last three days in Maine with the man she loved before their dad who just happened to show up at the bookstore. Will she tell Blake? Wonder what he'll have to say about it?*

Aidan looked at his watch. *I need to stop obsessing and get to the store.*

He drained his coffee cup, walked back to the house, locked up and headed for his truck. *It'll all work out. I just have to be patient.*

CHAPTER 35
GRACE AT HOME

Elise came in through the back door. She didn't expect to find her mother in the kitchen.

Grace was just as surprised to see her. "You're home early. Everything okay?"

"Everything's fine, Mom. Why do you always assume something's wrong?"

Grace didn't like her daughter's tone of voice. She attributed the bad mood Elise had been in all week to problems with Brian. Still, that was no excuse for being rude or disrespectful. Grace wanted to get to the bottom of it, but decided to ignore her behavior for the time being.

"I don't always assume something is wrong. I was merely asking a question. You're not usually home from work before five."

Carrying bags with both hands, she kicked the door shut with her foot. "I had some shopping to do."

"I can see that. Will you be home for dinner? Jimmy's cooking steak tips on the grill. I made a salad."

Elise shook her head. "I need to put these away." She hurried past Grace, stomped up the stairs and slammed her bedroom door.

Nothing wrong, my foot. We'll see about that. Grace went upstairs to her daughter's room and knocked on the door.

Elsie knew it wouldn't do any good to ignore her. "What do you want now?"

Grace took that as an invitation to enter and went right in. "I want to talk to you."

Elise continued to hang things in her closet. "Can't it wait?"

"No, young lady. It cannot."

Elise knew she had gone too far. Grace wouldn't let it go. "All right. What is it?"

"That's what I want to know from you. You've been acting strangely ever since I got home. You haven't had dinner with us all week and now you say you're not eating with us tonight either. I've been chalking the snide remarks up to you and Brian having another argument. But, I won't have you slamming doors and being out and out rude. Is Brian the problem, or are you angry at me for something?"

Elise didn't know how to answer her. She wasn't ready to get into what was bothering her with Grace. How could she tell her mother about finding the letter and reading part of it? How could she explain the thoughts going through her mind after reading her book again? She needed to sort it all out. Brian wasn't any help. He just told her what she did was wrong and that she should talk to her mother about it. If only she could talk to Jonathan. He always knew what to say to her. But, he was in Albany.

Elise hung up a skirt and turned toward Grace. "Some of it has to do with Brian. I really don't want to talk about it."

Grace didn't know what to say. "Some of it? So, there's more to it?"

"Mom, please. I need to figure out what to do about Brian on my own."

Grace gave up. She had her own drama going on that she needed to resolve. "Okay. But, I'm here if you want to talk." She walked out and closed the door behind her.

Later, once Elise had gone out, Grace called Aidan again and told him what had happened.

"How involved is she with this Brian?"

"It's hard to say. She's been dating him for the past five years. Tall, good-looking, polite, intelligent. Works in the family business. Jim thought a lot of him. I like him. Everybody does. He treats her like a queen. For a while, I thought it was becoming serious. Now, I don't know."

"I think you're right. There's something other than guy trouble bothering Elise. But, what could she be angry at you for?"

"I don't know. She's a bit moody at times, but we've always had a close relationship until…" Grace stopped in mid-sentence.

"Until what, Gracie?"

"Until her father died."

"That could be the crux of it. Unresolved feelings or feelings that were never dealt with can cause a lot of problems. Maybe she needs to talk to someone."

"She won't talk to me about whatever it is that's bothering her."

"I meant a professional. A counselor. Has she ever been to one? It helped Kelli a lot to talk to someone other than me or a girlfriend."

"Elise saw a counselor for several months, shortly after Jim passed. It seemed to help at the time. I thought she was doing much better. Now, I'm not so sure. I'm also not sure her current problem has anything to do with Jim."

"You think she's angry with you for something then?"

"Yes. But, I have no idea what it could be. I've been worried about how she'll take finding out about you, but I haven't even told her yet."

"I think it was good that you let her know you're there for her, but at the same time won't put up with the way she's been behaving."

"I hope so."

"It'll all surface sooner or later."

"I'm sure it will, but I've been home almost a week now."

Aidan was well aware of how long it had been since she left Maine. He called her every night and texted her during the day. "This long distance thing is tough. It's only been a few days, yet it seems like weeks. I miss you, Gracie. Talkin' on the phone's not enough. I want to hold you and kiss you."

"I know. I miss you too, especially at night, when I'm alone."

"When can we see each other again? Can you come up for the fourth of July?"

"I'd love to, but I can't go away on the 4th. There's too much going on around here. Besides, I haven't even told my kids about you yet."

Aidan didn't like that she hadn't told her family. He thought the sooner it was out in the open, the better off they'd both be. He knew he had to be careful not to push her too much on this.

"I understand why you haven't told them yet, but you have to do it sooner or later. You can't keep me hidden forever."

He made her laugh, but she knew he was right. "I plan to tell them this weekend."

"Great. Now, what's happening there on the 4th you can't miss?"

"We always have a family cookout. My mom makes her potato salad. The kids have a few friends over. We all go to the fireworks the night before."

"I could come there for the 4th. I'm good with a grill."

"Here?"

"Sure. Why not? I could stay at my dad's. He'd love it if I came there for a couple of days. I've been promising to do some things around the house for him anyway."

"I don't know, Aidan. Let me think about it for a couple of days. I'm sure the kids will be fine with it."

"I would have been just as worried about telling Kelli if she hadn't found out by accident."

"What about Kelli? Is she okay with it?"

"She was a little upset with me for trying to keep you a secret. But, she's happy for me."

"I'm glad to hear that. I told my friend Valerie today."

"What did she think?"

"She was a little skeptical. But, she's happy for me. I'm going to tell Jonathan tomorrow. I have a feeling he already knows."

"So you haven't told him yet?"

"No. He just got back from Albany. We're having lunch together."

Aidan hesitated. "Oh? What makes you think he already knows?"

"He's been talking to Charlene, remember?"

"Yeah, right."

"I'm sure he'll be happy for me too."

He didn't care what Jonathan Blake thought, but he knew Grace did. He was afraid an unfavorable opinion from him could cause a problem. *At least her girlfriend is in my corner.*

"Let me know how it goes with Blake. I'll call you tomorrow. 'Nite, Gracie."

Grace didn't tell Aidan everything about her talk with Valerie. Her friend was more than skeptical.

"You're not serious? Tell me you're not seriously thinking about a relationship with this man. And, a long distance one at that."

"Haven't you been telling me I need a man in my life again?"

"Yes, but I was thinking of someone like Jonathan, not one who dropped you and didn't have the decency to tell you why."

Grace had been best friends with Valerie Fitzgerald since she moved to Tucker's Landing fifteen years ago and opened her own real estate business in town. It was Val who sold Jonathan his house and referred him to Jim when he had a legal matter to settle. The five foot ten, raven-haired beauty had trust issues when it came to men ever since she caught her ex-husband cheating on her with one of his co-workers.

"We've been over this a hundred times. I'm not in love with Jonathan."

"But, you spend three days with a man you haven't seen in over two decades and you're in love?"

"I know it sounds crazy. Part of me has never stopped loving Aidan. I realized that when I came across my old journal and his letters in the attic months ago. When I got the idea to write about it, I thought it might give me the closure I needed. I never imagined he'd read it and come looking for me."

Valerie wasn't all that surprised. "I knew that story had a familiar ring to it! So he read your book, sent you anonymous roses, showed up at an author event and hid behind a book before getting up the nerve to talk to you?"

"He figured out who the book was really about. He wanted to know why I wrote it."

Grace told Valerie about her day in Ogunquit with Aidan and what happened at the lake. "I finally found out why he went away."

"I don't know if it's the craziest love story I've ever heard or the most romantic. I'd say you got more than closure. If you're happy, I'm happy. But, if he makes one wrong move, I'll hunt him down."

She hoped Jonathan would understand.

CHAPTER 36
LUNCH WITH JONATHAN

Jonathan was already seated when Grace arrived at the Portside Grill. He stood and greeted her with a big hug and kiss on the cheek.

"It's so good to see you. I've missed you."

"I've missed you too."

"You look fantastic. Maine must have agreed with you," he said, as he pulled out her chair.

"Thank you. How's your dad doing?"

"He's doing great."

"Your mom must be glad to have him home."

"Oh yeah. No one can take better care of him."

"It's a lot for her though. Does she have enough help?"

"He's got a visiting nurse and a home health aide. My sister's there every day. If I didn't think he was in excellent hands, I wouldn't have left, but it's good to be back. I have so much work to catch up on."

"I'm sure you do. The kids said to say hello. They're hoping you'll be over to see them soon."

"Of course. Maybe on the weekend. It must be nice having them both around."

"It is when they're home."

The waitress interrupted them. "Can I get you a beverage?"

Jonathan looked across the table. "A glass of wine?"

"I'll have a white Zinfandel, please and the Chicken Caesar Salad."

Jonathan laughed. "Looks like we're ready to order. I'll have the Fourteen Hands Merlot and a turkey club on rye. Light on the mayo."

When the waitress left, he looked at Grace. "Are you in a hurry?"

"No. Just hungry."

There was a lull in the conversation. Grace looked out at the incoming tide. It reminded her of dinner in Ogunquit with Aidan.

Jonathan thought she seemed preoccupied. He wanted to get her attention back to him. "This has always been one of my favorite restaurants."

Grace snapped back to the present. "Mine too. I'm glad we decided to come here today. And I'm glad you're home. Tell me what's going on with your book."

They talked about books, publishers and her kids through most of the meal. She held off telling him about Aidan for as long as she could.

"I know the author event went well. You hit it off with Charlene."

"Yes. She's very nice."

"You haven't told me about your vacation. How did you like Portland?"

Grace took a long sip of wine. "I never made it to Portland."

He held the last piece of his sandwich in mid air. "Oh? I thought you did a lot of shopping."

"I did, but not in Portland."

This is silly. I may as well come right out and tell him about Aidan. I'm sure he'll be happy for me. At least I hope so.

"Jonathan, I have something to tell you."

A concerned look came over his face. He finished the last bite, wiped his mouth with the napkin and reached for his wine. "What is it?"

"I ran into an old friend while I was in Maine."

"Someone from around here?"

"He used to be. He lives in Maine now?"

"How'd you happen to meet this old friend?"

Grace detected an edge in his voice. "He came to the bookstore."

"What a coincidence."

"It wasn't a coincidence. The event was well advertised. What is your problem?"

"I'm sorry if I overstepped. You have every right to go to dinner with an old friend."

"How did you know I went to dinner with him?"

Jonathan hadn't meant to let that slip out. "Didn't you?"

"Lunch and dinner, as a matter of fact. You haven't answered my question. How did you know I had dinner with him?"

"I just assumed. The guy sends you roses and goes out of his way to see you. It's a good guess he'd invite you to dinner."

He loosened his tie a little and looked at his watch. Jonathan always did that when he was nervous. "How did you know about the roses?"

He hadn't meant to say that either. Damn! "Didn't you tell me?"

She glared at him. "Charlene told you, didn't she? About the dinner and the flowers."

It took him a minute to answer. "Yes. She innocently asked me if I sent the roses. She assumed you told me about Aidan. I guessed the rest."

"You knew all this time? When we talked on the phone that night, you knew. Why didn't you say anything?"

"You didn't mention it either. I figured if you wanted me to know, you would have told me. Why didn't you tell me, Grace?"

She realized now that keeping it from Jonathan hurt him. "I don't know. It was late. I was tired and confused. I didn't think you'd understand. Besides, you needed to be thinking about your family, not me."

"Grace, is Aidan McRae the one you dated before you married Jim? The one who walked out on you?"

So he knew his name. She wondered how much Charlene told him and how much the woman knew about her three days with Aidan. "Yes."

"Then why would you go out with him? I could understand lunch maybe, but dinner too?"

"It's hard to explain, Jonathan. There were things I had to try to find out."

"And, did you?"

"Yes."

The waitress cleared the table and brought them the coffee they ordered.

Jonathan ran his hand over his hair and let out a big sigh. He poured cream into his cup. "Well, you got your answers. Now you can put it behind you and move on."

Grace took a sip of her coffee. "Not quite."

"What do you mean?"

"I mean I can't put it behind me, but I am moving on."

A confused look came over his face. "Okay, you lost me here."

"I can't put Aidan behind me."

Jonathan was afraid of her answer, but he had to ask. "What are you trying to say?"

She raised her eyes to meet his. "I'm in love with him."

"In love? You have a couple of meals with a guy you haven't seen in over twenty years and all of a sudden you're in love? What are you thinking?"

"We spent a lot of time together."

Before she could say anything else, he slammed his open hand down on the table, causing a few heads to turn. She couldn't believe his behavior. It wasn't like Jonathan to make a scene.

"Oh, come on Grace. You were only gone for three days! That's hardly enough time to fall in love. You got caught up in the past. See it for what it really is."

"I can see you aren't going to support me in this. I hoped you'd be happy for me. I'd better leave."

He was furious at himself for losing his temper. "Grace, wait. I'm sorry for getting so upset, but you're not thinking straight. You wrote a book about him. He showed up out of nowhere and all of a sudden, you're in love. You gotta admit, it sounds like something out of one of your books."

Grace was fuming. "Where did you get the idea my book was about Aidan? Oh wait, don't tell me. Charlene. How much did that woman just happen to let slip? And what right does she have suggesting such a thing?"

"Is she right? Is he Daniel?"

"What difference does it make?"

"How could you write about him? What would Jim think?"

That was a low blow. "Jim's gone. Nothing can bring him back. You told me yourself he'd want me to be happy."

"Not with that guy. How can you expect to have any kind of relationship with a guy who lives in the back woods of Maine? And what about your family? Have you thought of them? Have you told them yet?"

"For your information, he owns his own business and lives in a beautiful home on a lake. Of course I've considered my family. I plan to tell them in the next few days. Have you given any thought to how you're going to carry on a relationship with a bookstore owner from the back woods or were you just using her to get information?"

"You've been to his home?"

"Are you really worried about how Jim would feel, or do you have your own issues with this? What's really bothering you?"

"You slept with him, didn't you?"

He wished he could take the words back, but it was too late. "That is none of your business! I don't have to answer to you. I told you about Aidan because I thought we were friends and that you'd be happy for me. I can see I was wrong on both counts."

"Grace, I'm sorry. I shouldn't have said that."

She pulled two twenty dollar bills out of her purse, dropped them on the table and stood up to leave. "You're damn right you shouldn't have. I might be able to forgive you for that thoughtless remark, but not for trying to make me feel guilty about Jim or for loving someone again. Goodbye Jonathan."

People were staring, but Grace didn't care. She walked out of the restaurant leaving him to deal with the curious diners.

How could he be that insensitive? I never thought he'd react that way. What if he's right? What are my kids going to think? Damn him!

⇌

Jonathan sat dumfounded. *What did I just do? I can't believe I acted like such a jealous ass! I think she's making a huge mistake, but my actions were out of pure jealousy. I had no right to behave that way. I lost Nikki because of my foolish jealousy. I don't want to lose Grace. How am I going to get her to forgive me? Some friend I am.*

Ignoring the stares from other customers and staff, he motioned for the waitress to bring the check.

⇌

Grace sat in her car for a few minutes trying to calm down before driving home. She and Jonathan had their little spats, but never anything like this. She didn't think he'd be gung-ho happy for her, but she thought he'd at least support her like Valerie.

His words upset her terribly. It hurt knowing he had discussed her private business with Charlene. She blamed him more that Charlene. *I'm sure he led her to believe he already knew so she'd tell him what she knew.*

All the way home she kept hearing the ping of her phone. She wasn't about to pull over to see another text from him. She wanted nothing to do with Jonathan Blake.
I don't know if I can ever forgive him.

CHAPTER 37
ELISE AND JIMMY

Grace parked her car in the driveway and hurried into the house. She went straight to the kitchen and dropped her purse on the counter. Her keys fell out, slid across the granite and fell into the stainless steel sink. She opened cabinet doors, closing each one with a loud bang until she found the Advil. Grabbing a bottle of water from the fridge, she slammed it shut.

"What's all the commotion in here? Mom, are you okay?"

"Elise! You startled me. I didn't know anyone was home."

"I was in the living room. You blew right past me. What's going on?"

"I'm sorry. I didn't see you. I have a dreadful headache."

"Is that why Jonathan called asking if you got home okay?"

"He called?"

"Twice. Said you weren't answering his text messages."

Grace took a long swallow of water and sat down. "Did he say anything else?"

"Mom. What is going on? Did you two have a fight?"

I wonder if he told Elise anything. He wouldn't dare, would he? "Yes. We had a terrible argument."

"So that's why you weren't answering his messages."

"Yes."

"Over a little argument?"

"It was more than a little argument."

"I'm sure you overreacted. What could you two possibly have fought about that was that bad?"

Grace was in no mood for her daughter's allegiance to Jonathan. She popped an Advil in her mouth and took a long swallow of water. "Elise, for once, could you please take my side when it comes to Jonathan?"

"What's that supposed to mean?"

Jimmy came in through the back door. "I could hear you two outside. What's going on?"

Grace took another pill. She couldn't deal with Jonathan, a throbbing headache and them too. *Maybe I should sit them both down right now and tell them about Aidan. No. I need time to think.* Her phone pinged.

Elise looked at her mother. "She had an argument with Jonathan and now she won't even let him apologize."

Jimmy was relieved. "Is that all?"

"I have my reasons, Elise."

Jimmy knew better than to get between his mother and his sister, but he knew how Elise could be when it came to Jonathan. He gave his mother a hug. "It's okay, Mum. If he did something that upset you this much, let him sweat for a while."

Grace gave her son a kiss on the cheek. She could always count on Jimmy. "I should check my phone. It could be my publisher."

Elise continued to badger her mother. "Jonathan called twice before she got home. She won't even call him back. That's rude."

Jimmy didn't like the way Elise was behaving. She'd been in a bad mood ever since he got home. He thought it had something to do with a guy and brushed it off. Now, he wasn't so sure.

"Elise, back off. Whatever it is, it's between Mum and Jonathan."

Grace pulled her phone out of her purse. There were several messages from Jonathan. The last one was from Aidan.

How'd lunch go? Luv you.

She answered Aidan and ignored the others.

Can't talk now. Call you later. Luv you, too.

Elise gave her brother a smirk. "Good. You finally answered him."

"That wasn't him."

"What? I know he's sent you messages. Why are you being so mean to him?"

Grace didn't give her son a chance to intervene. She couldn't take any more of this. "Elise, sit down. You too, Jimmy. We need to have a talk."

Elise shrugged her shoulders and sat down. Jimmy pulled out a chair and sat close to his mother. "You don't have to tell us if you don't want to."

"Will you be quiet? Let her tell us."

Grace was taking hold of the situation now. It had gone way too far. She looked from one to the other. "That's enough. Both of you. This whole thing has gotten blown way out of proportion. Elise, I'll handle Jonathan in my own way and in my own time. But, that's not what I need to talk to you about."

CHAPTER 38
GRACE TELLS HER KIDS

Elise rolled her eyes and waited for Grace to speak. Jimmy turned sideways in his chair and faced his mother.

"What is it, Mum? You're not sick or anything, are you?"

Grace patted his hand. "Oh, no, Honey. Nothing like that. It's about when I was in Maine."

Elise was getting impatient. "But, Jonathan didn't go to Maine."

Jimmy had had about enough of his sister. "Elise, will you let her talk."

"It has nothing to do with Jonathan. This is about me." Grace hesitated before she continued. "I met someone while I was in Maine."

Elise was shocked. "What do you mean? A man?"

"Yes. A very nice one."

Jimmy was glad it wasn't bad news. "That's cool. How'd you meet him?"

"He came to the book signing. He invited me to dinner and offered to show me some antique stores in the area."

Elise didn't like what she was hearing. "You're telling us you went traipsing off to antique stores with a strange man and then out to dinner?"

"No, Elise. We went traipsing off the next day. We spent the day in Ogunquit."

"You spent an entire day with this guy?"

Jimmy tried to quiet his sister. "Pipe down, Elise. I think it's great. She deserves to find someone nice. Does he live in Maine?"

"Yes. He owns a hardware store in Casselton and has a lovely home on the lake."

Elise couldn't believe it. "You went to a strange man's home?"

"Aidan's not a stranger. He's an old friend. I knew him when I was in college. He's originally from here."

Elise glared at Grace. Jimmy asked a lot of questions. "He lives kind of far away. Do you plan to see him again? Does he have kids?"

Grace laughed. "You're going to make a good lawyer. He has a daughter. She's about a year older than Elise. Kelli lost her mother when she was six. She lives in Bridgeton with her boyfriend. They flip houses."

"That sounds interesting. You didn't answer about seeing him again, but I can tell you want to. When do we get to meet him?"

"I've invited him here for the 4th of July."

Elise pounded a fist on the table. "You invited that man here? In Daddy's house? How could you do such a thing? What were you thinking? What about Jonathan? He'll be at the cookout."

Grace couldn't take much more of her daughter's outbursts. She could understand her being upset, but she was totally out of control. Grace stood and faced her.

"Elise, there's no need to shout. I know you miss your dad. We all do. But, I'm still here and I'm entitled to a life. This is MY house. I have a right to have anyone I want visit me. I've always welcomed your friends. I expect you to do the same for me. If Aidan comes, he'll stay at his dad's home on Carlton Road, not here. Furthermore, Jonathan may not be coming to the cookout."

"That's what you two fought about, isn't it? You told him about Aidan McRae."

"How did you know his last name?"

"I know who he is. He's the one in the letter."

"What letter?"

"The one in your office."

Elise hadn't meant to let that slip out.

Grace wasn't sure which letter she meant, but she had a pretty good idea. She was furious at her daughter for reading her personal mail.

"You read my mail? That's why you've been behaving so strangely ever since I got home. Why didn't you just ask me, if you wanted to know about him?"

"I didn't know you were with him in Maine or that you intended to bring him here. I thought it was something from the past."

"You had no right to go snooping around my office!"

Jimmy had no idea what either of them was talking about. He wished they'd stop arguing.

"Elise, you're acting like a spoiled brat."

Elise stood up and lashed out at her brother. "And you're acting like a momma's boy!"

"A momma's boy! At least I don't go around reading other people's mail and throw temper tantrums when I don't get my own way. She's not gonna marry Jonathan! Get over it!"

"Fine. Have your boyfriend come here. But, don't expect me to like him."

Elise stormed out of the kitchen and out the front door, slamming it behind her. Grace rubbed her temples. For a minute, she forgot her son was still in the room. "My head's pounding. My daughter hates me. I may have just lost a good friend. I need to get out of here. I need to talk to Aidan. Maybe I should just take off and drive up to the lake."

Jimmy put an arm around his mother and tried to console her. "It's okay, Mum. It'll all work out."

"I'm sorry. I didn't mean to go on like that."

"This guy must mean a lot to you."

"He does, Jimmy. But, it doesn't mean I've forgotten your father. You know your dad and I dated in high school. When he went away to college, we went our separate ways. I met Aidan. We fell in love. He joined the Marines and ended up in Iraq. He was wounded. It was a difficult time for him. He broke it off and moved away."

Jimmy gave her a sympathetic look. "I know."

"What?"

"I did some yard work for his dad when I was in high school. He told me about his son and showed me pictures. You were in some of them. He told me the two of you dated and that you broke up when he came home. I met his granddaughter once when she was staying with him. She's pretty."

"You never told me this before."

"It was a long time ago. I didn't want to make you feel bad."

Grace squeezed her son's hand. "You're so much like your dad. I do miss him, you know, no matter what your sister thinks. But, I have to go on with my life. He'd want me to."

"I know, Mum. I'll talk to Elise. Don't worry. You know how she gets. She'll come around."

"I hope so, Jimmy. I miss Aidan and want him to be able to come for the 4th."

"Why wait? Why don't you take a ride up there now and see him? You know you want to."

"Now?"

"Sure. It will make you feel better and put some distance between you and Elise. It will also give me a chance to talk to her with you out of the house."

"You really think so?'

"Call him."

CHAPTER 39
CALL TO AIDAN

Grace tried to sound upbeat and cheerful when she called Aidan. "Hi. Are you still at work?"

He could tell she'd been crying. "No, actually, I'm home. Why, what's up?"

"You're home early. Going out?"

"No. I came home to do some paperwork. Is something wrong?"

Hearing his voice brought it all to the surface. She burst into tears. "Everything's wrong. I don't know what to do."

He turned off the tv and sat up straight on the couch. "What is it, Grace? Does it have to do with your lunch today with Jonathan? Please don't cry."

"That's only part of it."

"Try to calm down and tell me what happened."

"It was awful. I told him I was in love with you. He said terrible things to me. He even tried to make me feel guilty about Jim. I've never seen him act that way before. People were staring at us."

Damn that Blake! What in hell is wrong with him? I'd like to kick his ass. "What did you do?"

"He tried to apologize, but I walked out of the restaurant and left him sitting there."

"Good. Serves him right. You said he was only part of it. Did something else happen?"

"Yes." She wiped her eyes with a crumpled up tissue. "I told my kids about us."

Oh, oh. "It didn't go well?"

"I had a splitting headache when I got home. Elise told me Jonathan had called twice and said I wasn't answering his messages. She figured we had a fight and blamed me. I couldn't tell her what we fought about. It made her angry. We were arguing when Jimmy came in."

"Then what happened?"

"He tried to play referee and ended up in a battle with his sister. I couldn't take anymore. I decided it was time to tell them about you. I thought she'd understand why I was upset with Jonathan. I should have known better."

Aidan felt terrible. *I shouldn't have pushed her to tell them about me. I should have been more patient.* "How'd Jimmy take it?"

"He's happy for me. He wants to meet you. But, Elise is furious. She knew about you."

Aidan could feel his own anger toward Jonathan coming back. "How could she? Don't tell me Blake told her we were together in Maine. "

"She didn't know about that. She found an old love letter you sent me. When I mentioned your name, she pieced it together. Then, when I said I invited you for the fourth, she blew up at me and ran out of the house. Aidan, what am I going to do?"

Aidan ran his fingers through his hair. He wanted to take her pain away. "I'm so sorry, Sweetheart. I know how difficult girls can be at times. Is there anything I can do?"

"I could use a hug."

He wished he could hold her right now. "I'll get in my car and come there right now if you want me to."

Knowing he cared enough to do that, made Grace stop crying. "Thanks, but I'm afraid it would only cause more problems."

He wanted to hold her and comfort her. "I don't suppose you could come here."

"I thought you'd never ask."

"You mean it? You'll come here?"

"I can be there by seven, depending on the traffic. If you want me, that is."

Aidan leaned back on the couch and smiled. "Oh, Honey, I want you."

CHAPTER 40
BACK TO MAINE

Grace pulled a suitcase out of the closet, tossed it onto the bed and packed enough things to last through the weekend. *That should do it.* After a quick shower, she changed into a pair of comfortable jeans and gave her mother a call to let her know what had happened.

"I figured you should know in case Elise comes there. You're right. I can't let my kids run my life. I'm taking your advice. I've been given a second chance and I'm not going to blow it. Jimmy says he'll talk to Elise while I'm gone."

Janet Devlin wasn't surprised to hear any of it. Earlier in the week, her daughter told her about seeing Aidan in Maine. "I'd say Jonathan's a bit jealous. I'm sure he's sorry for acting so stupid. As for Elise, she thinks he can do no wrong. We both know that. She's headstrong, but she's a good kid. She'll come around. Tell Aidan I'm looking forward to seeing him at the cookout. Maybe he could bring his dad along."

"That's an idea. You two know each other, don't you?"

"Yes. We've been on a few committees together. Donald's an interesting man, not to mention handsome. Have a good time and don't worry about Elise or Jonathan. It'll all work out. You need to do what's right for you. Go for that second chance."

"Thanks, Mom. Talk to you soon."

Grace carried her suitcase, laptop and purse down the stairs and dropped them all in the foyer. She went into the den to say good-bye to Jimmy. He got up off the couch when his mother entered the room. "I'm leaving now. Here's Aidan's address and cell number. I won't be gone long. I'll keep in touch. Call or text me if you need anything. I called Gran and told her. She'll be around if you need her."

Jimmy hugged his mother. "Don't worry. I can handle Elise."

They walked back to the foyer together. He picked up the suitcase and walked Grace to her car. "Drive carefully. Text me when you get there."

Elise laughed at the way he sounded more like the parent than the child. "I will."

CHAPTER 41
GRACE AT AIDAN'S

Aidan was sitting in one of the wicker chairs on the front porch when Grace arrived. He practically jumped out of his seat the minute she pulled into the driveway. By the time she opened the door, he was standing there waiting to greet her.

His strong, welcoming arms made the long drive well worth it. She buried her face in his chest, hugging him as hard as she could. He could barely hear her muffled words. "I needed to see you. I feel better already."

"I was getting worried. Lotta traffic?"

"Yes. It brought my headache back. I stopped and took more Advil on the way here."

He lifted her head up and kissed her long and hard. "Does that help?"

"Immensely."

"Good. I have a lot more home remedies inside in case the Advil doesn't help."

"Then let's go inside."

He took her keys and popped the trunk. "Grab your purse from the front seat. I'll get the suitcase and laptop. You must be hungry."

"Now that you mention it, I haven't eaten since this afternoon."

"No wonder you have a headache. Let's get you fed."

She followed him into the house. "Don't go to any trouble."

"No trouble. I waited for you to eat. I have a Pinot Grigio chillin' in the fridge, fresh bread, sliced tomatoes and some of that chicken salad you like. Make yourself comfortable while I put your bags upstairs."

"That sounds wonderful."

Grace sent Jimmy a text to let him know she arrived safely and went into the downstairs bathroom to freshen up before dinner. When she came out, the table in the dining area was set for two. A candle flickered in the center. The sliders were open, letting in a cool, light breeze. Aidan was in the kitchen pouring two glasses of wine.

"Feel better?"

"Much, thanks. It's a long ride. Not like when we were kids and I went running to you with a problem. You were only ten minutes away then."

He laughed and handed her a glass. "I know. And the problems were smaller, even if they did seem earth shattering at the time."

He put an arm around her waist and led her to the sofa. "You just sit here and relax while I get dinner ready. It'll just take a few minutes."

"But, you always helped me find a solution."

He kissed her gently on the cheek. "We'll solve this one too. I don't know how yet, but we will."

Grace took a sip of her wine. "I hope so, Aidan. I really hope so."

"We'll work on that tomorrow. You've had a long, upsetting day. Tonight, I want you to relax and get rid of that headache."

He went into the kitchen, grabbed the rolls and wine off the counter and brought them to the table. He hated seeing her green eyes clouded with doubt. *I hope so too, Gracie.*

CHAPTER 42
FIRST NIGHT AT AIDAN'S

After dinner, Grace began to clear the table. Aidan pushed his chair back and got up. "I'll do that. You go sit on the couch."

She insisted on helping with the dishes. "I'm feeling much better. You were right. I needed to eat something."

He was glad to see some of the sparkle back in her beautiful eyes. "Okay. You clear the table. I'll put the food away and load the dishwasher." He blew out the candle. "But, then I want you to relax."

"What about you? Don't you go to bed early? I interrupted your work week."

Moving closer, he cupped her face with his hands and kissed her. "First of all, you are never an interruption. Secondly, I'm the boss. Sam can open the store, but I do have to go in for a little while. You can stay here and enjoy the peace and quiet. I can come get you so we can do a little grocery shopping, or I can pick up some things on my way home. You **are** planning to spend the weekend, aren't you?"

"Yes, if that's okay. I'd love to help with the groceries."

Aidan smiled. "Great. It's all settled then."

When the kitchen was cleaned up and the dishwasher started, they retreated to the living room. Aidan placed their glasses on an end table and turned on some soft music. He sat down next to Grace on the sofa and wrapped one arm around her shoulders.

She snuggled up against him and put her head on his shoulder. "This feels good. I missed you so much."

He buried his face in her hair, breathing in the sweet scent of her shampoo. "I missed you too. Modern technology is great, but texting and talking on the phone doesn't compare to this."

"I know what you mean."

He didn't want to get too into things tonight. "Have you given any thought to my coming to your house on the fourth?"

"Yes. I want you to come. Jimmy wants to meet you. Even my mother thinks you should come. She said to tell you she'd see you on the fourth."

"Your mother knows about us?"

Grace looked up at him. "I was going to tell you, but everything happened and I never got to it."

"She's okay with it?"

"She didn't like that you hurt her daughter, but she always liked you. She says second chances don't come often. I should listen to my heart, not my kids."

"Your mom's one smart lady. It can't hurt to have her in my corner."

"Mom thinks you should bring your dad along to the cookout. They know each other from being on town committees together."

"That's a thought. He might like that."

Grace sat up straight. She moved her head from side to side. "I'm getting a stiff neck."

Aidan leaned forward and started massaging her neck and shoulders. "Your muscles are all tight. Does this help?"

"It feels great. Is it a home remedy?"

"One of them," he said, kneading her shoulder blades with his hands. "Close your eyes."

As he rubbed from her neck down to her lower back, she felt the tension slowly dissipating, leaving her body totally relaxed.

Touching her excited him. "Feeling better?"

Rolling her head again, she leaned back against his strong hands. She didn't want him to stop. "Yes," she said, softly. "I can hardly wait to try some of your other remedies."

"Never keep a lady waiting."

In slow, steady motions, Aidan rubbed her shoulders, down her arms to her fingertips, back up to her shoulders then down her back. He slipped his hands under her shirt. The feel of her skin made him want more. Grace shuddered when he kissed her neck and gently began messaging her breasts.

When he stopped, it was because he had to have more of her. He turned her around and kissed her like he did that night in Ogunquit. They'd worry about their problems tomorrow. Tonight, was for them.

He stood up and held out his hand to her. "Let's go upstairs, Gracie."

Without saying a word, she took his hand and let him lead the way.

Aidan turned down the bed while Grace was in the bathroom changing. She came out wearing a short, black, silky pajama top.

"Forget your robe again?"

"I packed in kind of a hurry."

He gave her that mischievous grin of his and walked toward her. "That's okay. You won't need much."

Aidan held her face in his hands. "I love you, Gracie. We'll make it work."

She believed him. "I love you too, Aidan."

He kissed her, gently, at first. She wrapped her arms around his waist and leaned into him. He pulled her closer and kissed her again. She unbuttoned his shirt and kissed his bare chest. She liked the woodsy scent of his cologne. The touch of her lips excited him more.

He pulled off his shirt and tossed it in the corner. "You're killin' me."

"Want me to stop?"

"I want you in my bed. And tonight, you're staying all night. No running off, leaving me alone with my dreams this time.?

Aidan put his arms around her again. The silk felt cool on his skin. He undressed and led her to the edge of the bed. He lifted the silky top up over her head, dropped it at the foot of the bed and started kissing her neck and shoulders. "I want to kiss you all over."

She dug her fingernails into his muscular arms. He couldn't wait any longer. He had to have her. Now. Gently easing her onto the bed, he got in beside her and pulled the covers over them. He reached up and turned off the light. Holding her close, he pushed her hair behind her ear. "I'm gonna make love to you all night."

CHAPTER 43
ELISE AND JONATHAN

When Elise came home, Jimmy was in the kitchen eating pizza and reading the paper. "Where've you been?" he asked, without looking up.

"Gran's."

"I thought you might have gone to see Jonathan."

She knew he was trying to be subtle. *Mom's right. He is gonna make a good lawyer.* "He wasn't home."

"There's pizza."

Jimmy was a lot like their dad, even tempered, patient and never held a grudge. *He won't look at me, but at least he's speaking to me.* Elise sat down. "Thanks. I ate at Gran's."

"She's not home, in case you're wondering."

"I know. Gran told me she went to Maine."

Jimmy finally looked his sister in the eyes. "Can you blame her?"

Elise became defensive. "She didn't have to go running to him."

Loving Daniel

"You didn't have to go running to Jonathan, or Gran either, for that matter. What did Gran have to say?"

Elise turned and looked away for a minute, then back at her brother. "She tried to be diplomatic, but she took Mom's side."

"Of course she did. You'll never win an argument against Mum with Gran. She'll always defend her daughter."

"She said it's really none of my business. That's between Mom and Jonathan. She told me I should be happy for Mom. She also said I can't run my mother's life and gave me hell for reading even part of that damn letter."

"She's right there. How would you like it if Mum went into your room and read your diary? "

"I didn't go snooping in her office! I was looking for printer paper. The letter was on the floor. I picked it up. I thought it was a prop for a book. When I realized it was a letter to Mom, I stopped reading it."

"Then why did you get so upset when she mentioned his name?"

"Because he's the one who wrote the letter. He's Daniel. I feel like she's betraying Daddy by being with this guy again."

Jimmy was confused. "Who's Daniel? What are you talking about?"

"I forgot. You don't read her books. The last book she wrote, *Loving Daniel,* is really the story of her and this Aidan guy."

He began to understand where his sister was coming from a little, but still felt she was wrong. "Elise, you gotta let this go. Do you really want to destroy your relationship with your mother over an old letter? She deserves to be happy and she needs us to be happy for her."

Elise had to think about everything her grandmother and brother said. On some level, she knew they were right. She was suddenly relieved her mother was not home right now.

"But, she was mean to Jonathan. She wouldn't even give him a chance to apologize."

As usual, no one could get through to Elise where Jonathan was concerned. Jimmy threw his hands up in the air. "He acted like a jerk! He wasn't much of a friend when she needed him. He embarrassed her in public. I'd like to have a word or two with him myself, but we've got to let her deal with him."

Just then, the doorbell rang. Glad for the chance to end this conversation with her brother, Elise jumped up. "Finish eating. I'll get it."

When Elise peeked out and saw who was on the porch, she smiled and opened the door. "Jonathan! I'm so glad to see you."

Jimmy closed the cover on the pizza box. *Great. Just what I want right now.*

"Hi, Elise. May I come in?"

"Of course. Come on in. Can I get you anything? A glass of wine, coffee, a cold drink?"

"No. I'm all set. Thanks. Is your mother home?"

"No. Why don't we go in the living room and sit down?"

Jonathan had the feeling he wasn't going to like what Elise was about to tell him. "Is something wrong? Is Grace okay?"

"She's fine, but she's not home right now."

He followed her into the living room. "Maybe I will have coffee."

"Make yourself comfortable. I'll be right back."

When she went into the kitchen, Jimmy gave her a warning look. "Stay out of it. You'll only make things worse."

"Oh, Jimmy. He looks terrible."

"Elise, it's none of your business. Let them work it out."

Ignoring her brother, Elise made a cup of coffee for Jonathan and went back in the living room.

"Thanks," he said, taking the mug from her.

She sat next to him on the sofa. "I stopped by to see you earlier."

He took a sip of his coffee. "Oh?"

"I know you and my mother had an argument."

"She told you about it?"

"Not exactly. It didn't take much to figure it out. You called twice looking for her and said she wasn't answering your messages. She came home with a headache and all upset over something."

"Did she tell you what we argued about?"

"No. But, I figured that out too, once she told us about Aidan McRae. I tried to get her to call you or at least answer your text messages."

"She told you about Aidan?"

"Yes. She told Jimmy and me. I think what she did to you was mean and it was rude of her to ignore your calls."

Jonathan almost spilled his coffee. "Wait a minute. Wait a minute. Elise, you're way off base here. First of all, your mother doesn't have a mean bone in her body and you know it."

"But, she spent a lot of time with this old boyfriend of hers in Maine and then drops it on you at lunch. She should be apologizing to you."

"Honey, you've got this all wrong. I don't know what your mother told you, but the argument was my fault, not hers. I was totally out of line."

Elise was adamant. "No you weren't! She knows how you feel about her. Everyone does. It was very insensitive of her. And now she's bringing him here to the cookout."

"He's coming to the cookout?"

"Yes. And she said you may not be."

Jonathan rubbed his forehead.

Jimmy poked his head in. "Everything okay in here?"

Jonathan hadn't realized he was home. "Hi, Jim. How's it going?"

"Not good from the sound of the two of you."

"Oh, we're fine. I'm trying to set your sister straight on a few things."

"Good luck with that."

Elise stood up and looked at her brother. "Don't you have someplace you have to be?"

"First there are some things I want to say to Jonathan."

Elise folded her arms across her chest. "And you told me to butt out."

"It's okay. What's on your mind, Jim?"

Jimmy walked all the way into the room. "I don't know what happened today between you and my mom. It's really none of my business. But, I don't like seeing her upset like that. She didn't tell us much about the argument. She did tell us she met an old friend in Maine and had dinner with him."

"She spent a whole day with him!"

Loving Daniel

"Elise, I'm talking to Jonathan right now."

She sat back down, but kept her arms folded.

"Jimmy, it was all my fault. I acted like a jealous fool, which I had no right to do. She wouldn't let me apologize. She ran out of the restaurant and won't answer my calls. I don't blame her, but I do want to tell her how sorry I am. I hope I didn't ruin our friendship. I love your mom." Turning toward Elise, he added, "But, not in the way you think."

"But, Jonathan."

"Oh, I did, for a while. I finally realized it was one way and nothing would ever come of it. I settled for friendship and moved on a long time ago. When she told me about Aidan, I guess I was a bit jealous that it wasn't me. I stupidly let my feelings slip out. You know I date other women. In fact, I was thinking of bringing a date to the cookout. Your mom knows that."

Jimmy was glad he got his feelings out in the open with Jonathan. "So you don't have a problem with Aidan."

Jonathan got up off the couch. "No. My friend who owns the bookstore knows him well. She says he's a great guy."

Jimmy gave Jonathan a slap on the back and shook his hand. "Give Mum time. I'm sure you'll work it out. I'm late for a date right now."

"Okay, Jim. Thanks. By the way, where is Grace?"

Before Jimmy could answer, Elise turned toward Jonathan. "She's in Maine."

Jimmy wanted to strangle his sister. There was no need to tell Jonathan where their mother went. If she wanted him to know, she would have told him.

Jonathan didn't see that coming. *No wonder she's not answering my messages.* "Well, then. I guess we better all get used to Aidan McRae. I think he's going to be around for a while."

"I'm sorry, Jonathan. My sister doesn't always think before she speaks."

"He was gonna find out sooner or later."

"It wasn't up to you to tell him."

"It's okay, Jim. Don't keep your date waiting. I want to talk to Elise alone for a minute. You go on."

When Jimmy left, Jonathan turned toward Elise. "Your mom and dad were the first people I met when I came here. They welcomed me into their home. Your dad was my best friend."

Elise felt terrible. She hadn't meant to hurt him. *Jimmy's right. I don't think before I say something.* "I'm sorry. I shouldn't have told you."

"No, it's okay. And, I'm okay with your mom and Aidan. I've always had a special relationship with your mom because we're both writers. When Jim died, I grew closer to your mother. I missed him almost as much as she did. I think we turned to each other for comfort. Somewhere along the line, I fell in love with her. But, she wasn't in love with me. Eventually, I began to realize we were wrong for each other in that way and moved on. But, I still care a great deal for her."

Hot tears streamed down Elise's cheeks. "You don't have to tell me this."

"I want to. I've always felt like a part of this family. I've known you and your brother since you were children. I couldn't love you more if you were my own kids. I'll never forgive myself if I've done anything to ruin my friendship with your mother or with any of you."

She wiped the tears with the back of her hand. "She'll understand. Besides, I think she's angrier with me right now than she is with you. I blamed her for the argument you two had."

"Elise, that's wrong." He pulled a handkerchief out of his pocket and handed it to her. "I don't blame your mother and I don't want you to. You've got to stop taking my side against her. She's your mother. You'll never have a better friend or anyone who loves you as much as she does."

"I felt like she was betraying you. Then when I realized she knew him a long time ago, I felt she was betraying Daddy somehow."

"She's not betraying anyone, Honey. She's just moving on with her life. You'll understand that when you fall in love."

Elise stopped crying. She smiled at Jonathan. "Thank you. I'm sorry I caused so much trouble."

He gave her a hug. "It's good to see you smiling again. Now we both have to work on how we're going to get your mother to forgive us. I don't want to miss that cookout."

CHAPTER 44
FRIDAY AT AIDAN'S

Grace woke up to the scent of pine and a gentle breeze drifting through the open window. Birds chirped, breaking the early morning silence. *So this is country living.* She stretched her arms above her head, took a deep breath and let the tranquility wash over her.

After a few minutes, she got out of bed and walked over to the window. Peeking through the blinds, she could see Aidan on the deck. He was drinking coffee and reading the newspaper. She'd worry about their problems later. At that moment, all was right in her world. She wanted to enjoy it, if only for a little while.

Grace smelled coffee and bacon as soon as she opened the bedroom door. *I need some of that.* She showered in a hurry and went downstairs.

Aidan was at the stove. "Good morning."

She gave him a kiss on the cheek. "Good morning. Something smells wonderful."

"I take it you're hungry."

"Starving, but I need my coffee." Grace poured a cup for herself and gave him a refill.

"Sleep well?" he asked. "I didn't have the heart to wake you, as much as I wanted to."

"Very well, thank you."

"Breakfast will be ready in a few minutes. I thought we'd have it on the deck."

"I didn't get this kind of service at the Whittier Arms."

"I'll bet you didn't."

"I was talking about breakfast."

"Sure you were."

She helped him carry everything out to the deck. The sun was streaming through the trees. It promised to be a beautiful day. Grace watched a squirrel scurrying around on the ground below. "I think he smells the bacon."

"Don't give him any. He'll come back tomorrow for more. I know you think he's cute, but trust me, you don't want him up here with you."

"Oh, I know. It's beautiful here. And, peaceful. I'm happy I came, but I wish I hadn't brought so many problems with me."

He took one last swallow of coffee. "They're my problems too. When you're ready, we'll talk about everything that happened yesterday and figure out where we go from here."

"Not yet. I'm not good at problem solving this early in the day. I know you need to go to work. What time do you have to go in?"

"Not for a while. I talked to Sam. The shipment's coming in later than originally planned. I thought we could pick up a few groceries, have lunch and I'll go in later. If the order comes in on time, I should be home by three. You can stay here and relax or you can go into town if you like."

"Sounds good to me. I brought my laptop. I have some research I can be doing. How do you feel about Chicken Piccata?"

"What?"

"For dinner."

"I'm afraid it's not one of my specialties. I'm much better with things I can toss on the grill."

Grace laughed. "I meant do you like it. I'm going to cook you dinner for a change."

"Well, in that case, the kitchen's all yours, but tomorrow night I'm taking you out."

They cleaned up the breakfast dishes and headed for the grocery store. Grace got all the ingredients she needed to make her chicken dish and a salad. Aidan bought hamburgers, sausages and a couple of thick steaks. They picked up fresh rolls and a banana cream pie. "That ought to hold us for a while. We'll stop and get another bottle of wine."

―――

It was quiet with Aidan out of the house. Grace wasn't in the mood to do research. *It can wait.* Instead, she browsed through her email, texted Jimmy and called her mother.

"You were right, Grace. Elise came here. I tried to talk some sense into her. I don't know if it did any good."

"I haven't heard from her. I haven't texted her either. She'll come around when she's good and ready."

"Try not to worry. Whatever you do, don't back down. You're entitled to some happiness. Grab it while you can. Did you happen to mention bringing his dad to the cookout to Aidan?"

"He thinks it's a great idea. I'm pretty sure he's going to bring him along, if he doesn't have other plans. Talk to you soon."

She scrolled through her text messages to make sure she hadn't missed anything from Elise. There was a new one from Jonathan.

Kids told me what happened. Don't blame u for running away from home. Your friendship means the world to me. Please give me a chance to make it right between us.

She read it three times before responding.

I'm sure it was Elise who told you.

I had a long talk with her.

We'll talk when I get back.

That's all I ask.

Grace put her phone aside and started working on dinner. She made a salad, seasoned the chicken breasts, coated them with flour and put it all in the fridge. *All I'll have to do later is cook the chicken and pasta.* She smeared on sunscreen, tossed her hat, sunglasses and phone in a tote bag, grabbed a bottle of water and walked down to the Adirondack chairs.

The serenity of the lake had a soothing effect. Looking out over the calm water, Grace understood why Aidan came here to think.

Aidan was happy to find Grace relaxing down by the pier when he got home. He got himself a bottle of water and joined her.

He bent down and kissed her. "I see you're enjoying my favorite spot."

"Yes. It's inspirational. A quiet place to sort out your thoughts, too."

He sat down in the other chair. "Have you been doing that?"

"Yes."

"You want to talk about it now?"

"Yes."

Aidan positioned his chair so he could see her better. "Why don't you start with what happened at lunch yesterday."

"First, I think you should know Jonathan sent me another text message. I told him we'd talk when I get back."

He wasn't thrilled about it, but glad she told him. "Okay." He sat quietly and listened, while she told him how Jonathan reacted to her news.

When she was almost finished, Grace leaned forward and touched Aidan's arm. "He can be a bit hot tempered at times, but I've never seen him act like that before. He's usually very reserved, especially in public."

Aidan patted her hand. "I can see why you were so upset. He acted like a jealous fool."

"I know. But, he had no right to be jealous. And, he had no businesses discussing me with Charlene."

"What did you do?"

"He tried to apologize, but I wouldn't let him. I was angry and embarrassed. I put money down for my lunch and left him sitting there."

Aidan liked that she did that. "Good for you."

Grace sat back in her chair again. "When I got home, I had a splitting headache. I rushed into the house and didn't see Elise sitting in the living room. She came in to see what was wrong. Jonathan had called twice asking if I got home okay. Apparently, he told her I wasn't answering his text messages. She surmised we had a fight. When I admitted we had an argument, she immediately took his side."

"Without knowing what it was about?"

"My daughter worships that man. He became a father figure after Jim died."

"I guess that's understandable."

She told him how Jimmy heard them arguing all the way outside. "He came in and tried to intervene. Before I knew it, they were both going at it. That's when I decided to sit them down and tell them the whole story."

Aidan listened intently, waiting until she was done to comment.

"Wow. I'd forgotten how dramatic young girls can be. It sounds to me like she's torn between her father and Jonathan. If she sees him as a father figure, in her mind, it would be okay if you married him, but another man is a betrayal to both of them. Blake already fits in her world. There's no room in it for me or any other man."

"But, you have a place in my life and she's going to have to come to terms with it."

"It's not about your life, Gracie. It's about her life and she doesn't want anything, or anyone to change it. Her pain is still too raw from the last big change."

Grace reached into her tote bag and fished out a tissue. "I hadn't thought about it that way. She did idolize her dad. She thinks the world of Jonathan. What are we going to do?"

He leaned forward in his chair. "Maybe we just sit tight and give her some time to digest all this. I'm sure finding that letter confused her all the more. She couldn't deal with knowing you were in love with someone before her father. Then when you told her you were with me in Maine, she probably thought it was no coincidence and wondered if something had been going on when Jim was alive even. Who knows what went through her mind?"

She dried her eyes. "I have to admit, you make some good points. You're very intuitive."

He laughed. "Not really. I raised a daughter, remember."

Grace nodded. "And, did a great job of it."

Aidan reached over and put his hand on her arm. "I'll tell you another thing I learned about girls."

She was almost afraid to ask. "What's that?"

"They change their minds a lot."

He always knew how to make her laugh. "You're right about that."

He swatted at a mosquito. "Let's see what the next couple of days brings. It's getting late. How 'bout that dinner you promised me?"

CHAPTER 45
AIDAN'S NIGHTMARE

Aidan set the table while Grace prepared the meal. "There hasn't been a beautiful woman cooking in my kitchen since Kelli left home."

"Is Kelli a good cook?"

"Very good. She learned out of necessity at an early age. I worked a lot of hours. I didn't have time to be creative with meals. She decided we needed to expand our horizons where food was concerned and started experimenting. That kid makes one hell of an omelet."

Grace drained the spaghetti. "You're a good cook."

"Other than what I can toss on the grill, I'm pretty basic. That chicken smells great."

She handed him the grated cheese. "You can put that on the table and sit down. Everything will be ready in a few minutes."

Aidan hadn't enjoyed a meal so much in a long time. "This is fantastic. I could get used to this."

Grace smiled. "Thank you. It's nice for a change to cook for someone who isn't saying, 'chicken again' and rushing off to meet their friends."

After dinner, they retreated to the living room. Aidan flipped channels and watched TV, while Grace did a little of the research she neglected earlier. Not able to concentrate, she looked up from her laptop. "I gave some serious thought to what you said about both Jonathan and Elise."

He hoped she hadn't changed her mind and decided to go home. "And?"

"I agree with you. I think it's a good idea to distance myself from Elise for a few days. I only hope coming here doesn't antagonize her more. Jonathan mentioned he had a talk with her in his text. I'm not sure what he meant, exactly."

Aidan hated to admit Jonathan may have been trying to help. "Sounds like he might have been doing some damage control."

"I hope you're right. If there's one person my daughter will listen to, it's Jonathan."

He hugged her and kissed her cheek. "We'll work it all out. We're meant to be together. It's no accident we found each other again."

"You always know how to make me feel better."

"Put that laptop away and I promise I'll make you feel terrific."

Grace logged off and slipped her laptop back into its case. He turned off the TV, locked the sliders and blew out the candle. She followed him upstairs. Aidan kept his promise.

Exhausted as she was, Grace had trouble sleeping. Aidan's tossing and turning kept her awake. He talked in his sleep, but she couldn't make out the words. *Poor thing must be having a bad dream.* When he quieted down, she drifted back to sleep, until his screaming awakened her.

"NOOOOO!" Aidan bolted straight up in the bed.

Her heart pounded as she sat up and turned toward him. "Aidan, you're having a bad dream."

There was a look of sheer terror in his eyes. He didn't seem to be fully awake. His tee shirt was drenched from sweat. This was more than a bad dream. It frightened her. She'd heard stories about people with PTSD having terrible nightmares. He told her he had anxiety problems and flashbacks, but not about nightmares. He never liked to talk about it, so she didn't push it.

"Aidan, wake up. You're okay. It's just a dream."

He looked around the room, then at Grace. Her voice brought him back to the present. "Gracie."

"I'm here, Aidan. You're safe."

He was breathing heavy. "I'm so sorry you had to see that. I must have scared the hell out of you."

"Only because I had no idea. Is there anything I can do or something I can get you?"

He needed a few minutes to pull himself together. "I could use a bottle of cold water. Maybe two."

"I'll be right back."

Aidan knew he should have told her about his dreams. *It was unfair of me not to tell her. She has a right to know what she's getting into. What will I do if she decides she can't deal with it?*

Grace came back into the bedroom with two bottles of water for Aidan and one for herself. He had stripped the sheets off the bed and was putting on clean ones.

"Here, drink your water. I'll finish that."

He sat in the chair in the corner of the room. "I should have told you about all this."

"Why didn't you?"

"I don't know. Partly because I was embarrassed to tell you and partly because I was afraid if you knew how I get sometimes, it would scare you off."

She smoothed out the top sheet, walked over to where he was sitting and knelt down in front of him. "We're not kids anymore, Aidan. It can't always be you solving my problems. We're both coming into this relationship with baggage. We have to accept the whole package for it to work."

He finished the first bottle of water. "You're right."

She moved over to the bed as he began to speak.

"I've been pretty lucky. I never turned to alcohol or drugs, although there was a brief period when I drank a lot more than I should. That was when I first left home. I get moody, but not depressed like I used to."

He paused to open the second bottle of water. "I went to therapy for a long time. It helped. Kelli made a big difference in my life, especially after her mother died and she came to live with me. She gave me a purpose in life again. I concentrated on giving her a good home."

"I keep busy with work and go to the gym. The nightmares have been the worst of it. They've been less frequent the past few years, but every now and then, one pops up and you saw what that was like."

Grace wondered what could have caused it. "Do you have any idea what triggers them?"

"Sometimes stress or being overtired. I work a lot of hours. It can be a news event. I was getting them a lot right after 911."

"I already mentioned I take medication for anxiety. I still get anxious and have an occasional panic attack, but it's nowhere near as bad as it used to be. I've been known to freak out over loud unexpected noises and it's never a good idea to sneak up on me."

She leaned back against the pillow, but didn't say anything.

He figured she had to be getting pretty tired. It was close to dawn. "So, that's the whole package. Do you think you can handle a guy like me?"

Grace got up and walked over to the chair. She leaned over and kissed him. "I think together, the two of us can handle anything."

CHAPTER 46
KELLI AND GRACE

Grace woke up at 8:00 a.m. on Saturday. She needed coffee. Not wanting to disturb Aidan, she grabbed her clothes, slipped out of the room and into the bathroom. She brushed her teeth, pulled her hair into a ponytail, got dressed and tiptoed down the stairs.

When the coffee was ready, Grace poured herself a cup, got her laptop and went out on the deck. It was quiet. She sat under the umbrella, shaded from the bright sun peeking through the trees. *No wonder he loves living here.* She logged on, took a sip of coffee and typed in PTSD.

She didn't hear Aidan in the kitchen or notice him watching her from the doorway. "You're up early, considering I kept you awake half the night."

His voice broke her concentration and made her jump. "I didn't know you were up. Good morning."

He opened the screen door and walked out onto the deck. "Sorry. I didn't mean to startle you."

"I woke up about an hour ago. Thought I'd let you sleep."

"Thanks. I needed it." He kissed her and sat down. "Thanks for making the coffee too."

"You're welcome. I could use another cup. Be right back."

Aidan watched her go inside. He liked that she felt comfortable enough to make herself at home.

When Grace came back out, she shut down her laptop. "I can see why you love living here. It's beautiful."

He smiled, remembering something she said on her first visit. "It's a writer's paradise."

She laughed. "Romance writers love stories that take place near a lake."

"Maybe you'll write one about here."

"Don't think I haven't thought about it."

He looked down at the table for a minute, then back up at her. "About last night. I'm sorry you had to see that, but I'm glad you know, now."

She reached out and touched his hand. "Me too."

"You were researching it weren't you?"

I never could fool him for a minute. "I hope you're not angry."

"Of course not. I love you for caring enough to try to understand it."

To lighten the mood again, he changed the subject. "I'm thinking we might hang around here today and relax. Unless there's something you'd like to do, of course. Kelli and Todd come by sometimes on Saturday when I'm not working. But, I can tell her I'm busy. Then tonight, I'll take you out to dinner."

"It all sounds good to me. It would be nice to see Kelli again and meet her boyfriend. But, you should probably let her know you have a house guest."

"I'll do that."

"I'm going upstairs to shower."

"Okay. I'll read the paper for a while, then start breakfast."

Aidan followed her into the house. He came back out with a second cup of coffee, the newspaper and his phone. He sent Kelli a text letting her know he had company and invited her to stop by with Todd.

After breakfast, Aidan went back to reading the newspaper. Grace played around with a story idea and took pictures of the lake and the squirrel as he scuttled from tree to tree. When they got hungry again, she made sandwiches with the rest of the chicken salad and brought them outside.

"Country air must increase the appetite. I never eat like this at home."

He stood and took the plates from her. Before she sat back down, he wrapped his arms around her and started kissing her neck. "Did you ever think it might be from all the exercise?"

"You think so?"

He nibbled at her ear. "Ya, but the good thing is, my exercise program burns calories."

"Ah. Would you like us to come back later, Dad?"

Aidan pulled away from Grace so quickly he almost fell over backwards. "Kelli. Todd. No, it's okay. Come on up on the deck. We didn't hear you pull up."

"You didn't answer the door so we came around to the back."

"We were just about to have lunch."

Kelli couldn't help laughing. "We can see that."

Grace regained her composure. "It's good to see you again, Kelli. Won't you join us?"

Kelli and her boyfriend climbed the stairs onto the deck. "Thanks, but we had lunch. It's nice to see you again too, Grace. This is Todd Curtis. Todd this is my dad's friend, Grace Madden."

He shook her hand. "Nice to meet you, Ms. Madden."

Todd reminded her of Elise's boyfriend. He had the same boyish smile and sandy blonde hair as Brian, but Todd was a little taller and broader through the shoulders. They both had muscular arms from working out regularly.

"Please, call me Grace. Can I get you a cold drink?"

Kelli answered for him. "I'll get it. We brought beer. Would you like one, Grace?"

"No, thank you."

"Daddy?"

"I'm all set."

Kelli came back out with a beer for Todd and water for herself. He was talking to her dad. "Damn thing died on me yesterday. I went to buy a new one last night. The one I want is out of stock. I had 'em order it, but it won't be in until Wednesday. If I could borrow yours till then, I'd appreciate it."

"No problem, but I'll need it back by Friday. I promised my father I'd replace a broken step on his back porch. I'm leaving early Saturday morning."

"You're going to visit Grandpa?" Kelli asked.

Aidan looked at Grace, then back at his daughter. "Actually, I'm going to a cookout at Grace's on the 4th, but I'm staying at your grandfather's."

"Oh. Well, I'm sure he'll be happy to see you."

"I want to get that step replaced before he falls and breaks a hip or something. What are you guys up to for the 4th?"

He looked at Brian. "Your parents having their annual cookout?"

"Oh, ya. They'll be disappointed you won't be there, but they'll understand."

Aidan was glad he was off the hook on that one. He liked Brian's family, but he hated having to go to any social events at their home. There always seemed to be an "extra" female guest he just "had" to meet.

"Tell them I said thanks for the invite. Listen, I have to run by the store to check on a few things. How 'bout taking a ride with me? Gracie, you don't mind, do you?"

"Of course not."

"We won't be long."

Grace was nervous about being alone with his daughter. She wasn't sure how Kelli felt about her dad having weekend guests. "Take your time."

When they left, she turned toward Kelli. "I could use that beer now."

"Me too."

Kelli came back with two beers. "Why don't we drink them down by the water?"

"Okay."

The two women sat in the Adirondack chairs drinking beer and looking out at the lake.

Grace spoke first. "I'm sorry if I messed up your plans for the 4th. Your dad didn't mention a previous engagement. I probably put him in a tough position."

"Are you kidding? He hates going to that cookout. Brian's mother is always trying to fix him up with one of her relatives. He just goes for me."

Grace wasn't sure how to respond. "Well, in that case, I don't feel so bad."

Kelli laughed. "Don't. He'd much rather be with you. Anyone can see that. I'm glad he's going to visit my grandfather."

"As a matter of fact, your grandfather's coming to the cookout."

"He is?"

"Yes. It was my mother's idea. She and Donald know each other from serving on various committees together. My son knows him too. Jimmy used to do yard work for him when he was in high school."

Kelli smiled. "Little Jimmy. I remember him. He used to mow the lawn and cut back the hedges. Nice kid."

"I didn't even know about it until recently. He remembers you too. He told me he met you there once."

Yes. Several times, in fact. Grandpa liked Jimmy. He'd listen to him go on about my grandmother and my dad. He even sat there and looked at old photo albums. I was bored. I'd seen them a hundred times, but Jimmy seemed genuinely interested."

Kelli looked down at the ground. "You were in some of those pictures. I remember now."

Grace reached over and put a hand on Kelli's arm. "Does it upset you?"

"No, not anymore. I just hadn't put it together until you mentioned Jimmy. I used to wonder about the woman in the pictures with my dad and what happened between them. He doesn't talk much about when he was younger. I learned what little I know from my grandfather."

"Some things are just too painful for him to talk about."

Kelli looked up at her again. "It's hard to picture him in high school or having a girlfriend. How'd you meet him?"

Grace put the half empty bottle on the table and sat back in the chair. "He was a year ahead of me. I didn't really know him then. He was pretty popular with the girls. We started dating in college. My car broke down one night. Your dad towed me to the garage where he worked at the time. He asked me out that same night."

"He didn't waste any time, did he?"

"No. He was impatient, even then."

They both laughed.

Grace shifted in her chair. "So, you're really okay with your dad and me?"

"I won't lie to you. I was a little upset at first. Nothing personal against you. I would have felt the same about any woman. But, then I thought about how happy I am. My dad worked hard so I could have a good life. I never heard him complain about it, either. A lot of men wouldn't have taken on a six-year old. He deserves to be happy."

Grace fought back tears. "I wish my family felt the way you do."

"Your kids aren't on board with all this yet?"

"Jimmy is. He's been very supportive. It's my daughter. Elise feels I'm being disloyal to her father."

"It's natural to feel that way. Elise had her father the whole time she was growing up. I only had my mom for six years. I have very few memories of her and none of my parents together. They divorced when I was two. Yet, when he started dating Charlene, I felt he was betraying my mom somehow. Elise is probably having a hard time with it because you guys have a history and you wrote a book about it."

Grace knocked over her empty bottle. "Is there anyone who hasn't read that book?"

"I'm sorry. I shouldn't have said that."

Grace pushed her hair back. "It's okay. You're probably right. Elise found one of your father's old love letters. She didn't read the whole thing, just enough to figure it out. Who knows what she's thinking?"

Grace heard Aidan's voice coming from the deck. "Sounds like our guys are back."

Kelli touched Grace's hand. "Don't worry. Elise will come around. She isn't going to chance losing her mother too."

It was 3:30 by the time the kids left. "Everything go all right with Kelli?"

"Yes. We had a nice talk. She's a smart young lady."

"That she is."

"I'm tired. Would you mind if I take a nap before we go to dinner?"

Aidan kissed her cheek. "You must be exhausted after last night. I've got a few things to do in the shed. I'll wake you in about an hour."

Grace fell right to sleep. She dreamed of Aidan. They were kids again, in the gazebo, holding hands and laughing. When she woke up, he was standing over her. "Well at least one of us has pleasant dreams."

Grace was confused. "What?"

"You were smiling."

"I was dreaming about us. We were in the gazebo."

He sat on the edge of the bed. "Maybe we can sneak over to your mom's next weekend. I'd like to sit in the gazebo with you like we used to."

She raised herself up on her elbows. "I'm sure we can work it in. How much time do we have before dinner?"

He pulled her up against him. "Plenty."

CHAPTER 47
AT THE BLUE ANCHOR

The Blue Anchor was crowded. The manager came right over when he saw Aidan.

"Nice to see you, Aidan."

The two men shook hands. "Hey, Gregg. Good to see you, too. This is my friend, Grace Madden."

"Welcome to the Blue Anchor. I'll have a table for you in about ten minutes."

"Thanks."

Grace gave him a nudge. "I'm impressed."

He whispered in her ear. "You're not the only celebrity in town."

Grace liked the atmosphere. A big blue anchor was on the wall next to where the hostess stood. A giant, carved wooden fish hung over the long, u-shaped bar. The dark blue walls in the dining room were decorated with paintings of ships at sea and ocean scenes. "This is nice. I love a nautical theme."

"I thought you would. They have entertainment on the weekends."

A few minutes later, Gregg came back with menus and personally led them to a corner table in the main dining room. "Enjoy your dinner."

Grace looked at her menu. "So many good choices. I don't know what to order."

"Seafood's their specialty, but they also do a good prime rib. That's what I'm getting."

After changing her mind several times, Grace decided on the prime rib as well. The waitress brought their drinks and rolls. They were buttering their bread. Aidan was telling her about the band that was setting up for later. He didn't notice the woman approaching them.

"Aidan! Hi. I thought that was you."

He knew who it was before he even looked up. "Charlene. Hi. What are you doing here?"

"Same as you. Hello, Grace. Nice to see you."

Grace forced a smile. "Hello, Charlene."

Aidan couldn't believe it. *Of all the nights for her to come here.* "Who are you here with?"

"Mark. We're celebrating his new job. He got promoted to Assistant Manager at the bank."

Aidan waved to a young man on the other side of the room. "Mark is Charlene's son. Bring him by to say hello after dinner. I'd like to congratulate him."

Grace remembered he told her Charlene had a son. "Yes. I'd love to meet him."

"I will. You two enjoy your evening. We'll stop by before we leave. I know he wants to say hello."

The waitress brought their salads. Aidan hoped he hadn't upset Grace by asking Charlene to bring her son over, but he did want to see him. "I had no idea she'd be here."

"Of course you didn't. Don't worry about it."

Dinner was every bit as good as Aidan told her it would be. Grace went to the ladies room before their coffee and dessert came. Aidan looked up and saw Charlene go in shortly after her. *Oh, oh. That's no coincidence. What in hell is she up to?* He sat, drumming his fingers on the table.

Grace was re-applying her lipstick when Charlene walked in. "Grace, can I speak to you for a minute, please?"

After an awkward pause, Grace managed a smile. "What's on your mind?"

"I'll get right to the point. Aidan probably saw me come in here. I could see bumping into me made him nervous. I want to apologize for any trouble I caused between you and Jonathan. I assumed you told him you had lunch with Aidan. I never would have mentioned it otherwise."

"I take it he told you about our argument."

"Yes. He was terribly upset. If it's worth anything, I let him know he behaved like a jerk. I told him I don't want to go out with him if he has feelings for you. He said the two of you were good friends, nothing more."

"That is true. Believe me, Jonathan had no right to act the way he did and he knows it. I'm sure he was mostly to blame. I accused him of using you to get information about Aidan and me."

"He seems really sorry. I'd like to give him another chance, but I'm still thinking about it. He mentioned a cookout at your house. Now, he's worried he won't be welcome there."

"I told him we'd talk when I get home. We'll straighten things out. He's really a good man."

"I hope we can all be friends. I'd still like to have the two of you for an author event."

Grace dropped her lipstick back in her purse. "I'd like that too."

"So you forgive me?"

Grace smiled at Charlene. "Yes, I forgive you. Think about giving Jonathan another chance. I'd love it if you'd come to the cookout with him."

"I'd love to, if he still wants me to."

"I'm sure he does. I'd better get back out there. I don't want my dessert to melt."

When Grace got back to the table, the waitress was just bringing their desserts. "That looks wonderful."

He waited until the girl poured the coffee and left. "Are you gonna tell me what happened in there?"

She reached for the sugar. "Relax, Aidan. Everything's fine. Charlene apologized for telling Jonathan about our lunch date. We talked. I realized it was more his fault than hers. I don't think she did it out of spite. I know him. He pumped her for information."

"I'm glad you two talked. Anything else?"

She took a sip of coffee. "Yes. I invited her to the cookout."

Aidan thought he heard her wrong. "Did you say you invited her to your house next weekend?"

"Well, he did ask her earlier. Assuming Jonathan and I will get things straightened out between us, I don't see why he shouldn't bring her."

"You'll work it out. Now, eat your dessert. And, take your time. The band will be on soon. I want to dance with you."

CHAPTER 48
GRACE GOES HOME

Sunday was a warm, sunny day. Tired from their evening out, Grace and Aidan enjoyed a leisurely morning. They went for a swim and had a light lunch out on the deck before she left for home around two o'clock.

Aidan carried her suitcase and laptop out to the car. "It's been a great weekend, despite the problems. I hate seeing you leave."

"I'm glad I came. I feel better about things now. You always make me feel better. I hate to leave too, but we both know I have to."

"I know." He held her and kissed her until she broke away. "I have to make it last."

"Well, we have the 4th of July to look forward to."

He smiled at the thought of it. "Be careful driving home. Text me when you get there."

The house was empty when Grace got home late Sunday afternoon. Jimmy sent her a text earlier letting her know he was going to a Red Sox game and wouldn't be home until late. She still had not heard from Elise and had no idea where her daughter might be.

She texted Aidan.

I'm home. Miss u already. luv u. ttyl.

Luv u 2. Call u tonight. Looking forward to weekend.

Grace brought her suitcase and laptop upstairs, unpacked and tossed in a load of laundry. She went into her office, took out her list of things to do for the cookout and headed back downstairs.

The kitchen was spotless. She wondered who was responsible for that. It wasn't like Jimmy to clean the kitchen.

Elise came in the back door. "Did you just get home?"

"About an hour ago."

"Jonathan was here the other day."

Grace wasn't sure how she should respond, but decided to be honest with her daughter. "I know. He texted me."

"You answered him?"

"Yes. We're going to talk. He's coming for coffee tomorrow."

"That's good."

"Elise, I don't want you getting any wrong ideas. Neither of us wants to lose the friendship we have between us."

"Does that mean he's coming to the cookout?"

"I don't know yet, but probably. I'd like him to."

"Is Aidan coming?"

"Yes."

Elise wasn't happy about it, but she knew there was nothing she could do to change things. *This ought to be interesting.*

Grace tried to change the subject. "Thank you for cleaning the kitchen."

"You're welcome. Jimmy left it a mess, as usual."

Grace laughed. "Housework's never been his thing."

"Well, I need to go change. Brian's picking me up in a half hour. We're going to grab something for supper and then to a movie."

"Have a good time."

Grace could still feel Elise's hostility. *At least she's talking to me. It's a start. Aidan was right about keeping my distance for a few days. Now, to tackle Jonathan.*

CHAPTER 49
THE APOLOGY

Jimmy was about to get into his car when he saw Jonathan pull into the driveway in his black BMW. He walked over to the car and waited for him to get out.

"Hey, Jonathan. Good to see ya."

Jonathan shook Jimmy's hand. "Hi, Jim. How's it going?"

"Great. Mum's in the kitchen. Go on around to the back door. She's expecting you. I'll be out for the rest of the morning. Elise is working."

Jonathan smiled. *Jimmy's looking more like his dad every day.* "Thanks."

Jimmy pointed to the back seat. "Forgetting something?"

"What?" Jonathan turned quickly and looked inside his car. "Oh! The flowers! Good thing you noticed."

Jimmy laughed as he walked toward his car. "Good luck with Mum. She's in a good mood. I'm sure we'll see you at the cookout."

A few days in Maine must have done her good. "I hope so."

Carrying the bouquet of flowers, he headed to the back of the house.

Grace was waiting at the door. "Hi. Come on in."

"Hello Grace."

Like a kid on his first prom date, he stood there holding the flowers, unsure of what to do next.

Trying to get past the awkwardness, she smiled. "Are those for me?"

He stammered. "Oh…yes…I, I thought it might help if I came bearing gifts."

"You didn't have to do that, but they're lovely. Such pretty colors. Sit down while I put them in water. I'll get us coffee and we can talk."

Jimmy was right. She does seem to be in a good mood.

Grace came back with two cups of coffee and a plate of pastries. "So, you mentioned you spoke to Elise."

"Yes. I don't know how much good it did, but I tried."

"Well, I appreciate it."

"Have things been any better between the two of you since you've been home?"

"Somewhat. We're speaking to each other. Sort of an unspoken truce. But, things still aren't right. A lot needs to be resolved. We need to really talk about it. With Elise, it will be when she's ready. You know how that goes. I hope she doesn't ruin the entire holiday weekend for everyone. She's not happy I've invited Aidan."

"Look, Grace, before you go any further, there are some things I need to say."

"Okay."

"First of all, you haven't let me apologize. Text messages and flowers aren't enough. You deserve better. You need the words. Face to face. That whole episode at the Portside was entirely my fault. I acted like a jealous ass."

Grace interrupted him. "I know you were jealous, but I thought all that was behind us."

"It is. I had no right to act that way and I know it. I wasn't jealous of Aidan, exactly. I don't even know the guy. I was upset because it wasn't me you fell in love with. The truth is, I would have been upset no matter who it was. Am I making any sense?"

Grace did understand him. They always understood each other. "I think so. I'd never seen you like that before. I've seen you get angry, but it was never directed at me. I didn't know how to handle it."

"I know. My jealous tantrums cost me a lot in the past. I've mellowed over the years, but when I lose it, I really lose it. I'm sorry for scaring you and for embarrassing you, especially in a public place. I'd never want to do anything to destroy our friendship."

"Oh, Jonathan, I know you wouldn't. Maybe I overreacted."

He covered her hand with his and leaned toward her. "No, you didn't. I had no right to try to make you feel guilty about Jim. No right at all. He'd be the first one to tell you to go on with your life. He'd want you to be happy. Does Aidan make you happy, Grace?"

"Yes, Jonathan, he does. But, now I have this mess with Elise to contend with and a houseful of people coming on the weekend."

"I'll talk to Elise again. She'll come around. I'm sure once she gets to know Aidan, she'll feel differently."

"I'm sure you will too when you get to know him."

"Charlene says he's a great guy." *Damn, I'm stupid.* "I'm sorry. I shouldn't have brought up Charlene."

"Why? You're not planning on bringing someone else to the cookout are you?"

"No, but I didn't think you'd want me to bring her, under the circumstances. I know you think she deliberately fed me information, but I wheedled it out of her."

Grace shook her head. "Well, now I'm in another embarrassing position thanks to you."

"How's that?"

"Didn't she tell you Aidan and I ran into her Saturday night?"

"No. What happened?"

Grace gave him an innocent look. "I invited her to the cookout. Will it be a problem?

Jonathan leaned forward and kissed her. "Grace Madden, you are something else."

CHAPTER 50
DONALD

Donald McRae was looking forward to the weekend. He went out early Saturday morning to buy groceries and stopped by Mia's Bakery to get an apple pie. His son hadn't been home to visit in months. He wanted everything to be just right.

After putting away the food, he tidied up the kitchen, tucked the photo albums in the closet and went out on the porch. He grabbed the big green watering can and tended to his flowers while he waited for Aidan.

When he was still employed, his job at the bank kept him out most nights at work-related or civic events. His involvement in the community helped ease the loneliness after losing his wife, Emma, six years ago to cancer. Once he retired, the social engagements lessened. He was lonely in the big house on Carlton Road.

Aidan asked him to move to Maine, but he didn't want to leave Tucker's Landing, the town he'd lived in all his life.

"I'd miss my friends and my weekly poker games. Thank you son, but my home is here. Keep my room ready. I'll drive up for a visit once in a while."

Aidan understood his dad's reasons for not wanting to make a move. "The offer's always open if you change your mind."

Donald began volunteering at the Tucker's Landing Senior Center a couple of days a week. Between gardening, his work at the center and being on several committees, he had little time to dwell on missing Emma.

He dated occasionally, but there was only one woman in town he had any real interest in. Janet Devlin. They were on a couple of committees together over the past few years and both volunteered at the senior center. *She's a classy lady and just as pretty as she was when Aidan dated her daughter Grace.* He wanted to ask her out, but was afraid of putting her in an awkward position with her daughter.

One night he gave Janet a ride home from a meeting. She invited him in for coffee. Being a widow, she understood what it's like to lose a spouse.

"It never seems to get any easier, does it? Time passes. Life goes on. But, we never stop remembering."

He touched her hand, leaving it there longer than necessary. "That's not a bad thing. Would you want to forget them?"

"No, of course not. I never thought about it like that."

"Remembering is good. We just have to learn to keep it in its perspective so we can go on with our lives. It's what they'd want us to do."

As he watered his bright red geraniums, Donald thought about his son. He served his country, raised a daughter alone, built a business from the ground up and made a good living. They butted heads many times while Aidan was growing up because of his independent nature, especially when it came to his education. He didn't want his parents taking out a second mortgage on their house to pay for college. He got a job in a garage and took night courses at Salem State. They paid for books and a few incidentals that came up.

As he continued to water, Donald thought about the way things happen in life. *Maybe now that Aidan's gotten back with the Devlin girl, I'll get to see more of my son. And...who knows, I might finally ask her mother for a date.*

CHAPTER 51
AIDAN ARRIVES

For the first time in years, Aidan drove down the streets of Tucker's Landing without having to avoid places too painful to remember. The good things about his hometown came back to him. He went by the football field, the movie theater and the spot where Grace's car had broken down. He rode along the beach and thought about the happy times he had there with Grace. *Maybe we'll have time for a walk on the beach later today or tomorrow.*

On impulse, Aidan drove by Grace's childhood home. Janet Devlin was getting out of her car. As she turned and he got a better look at her, he couldn't help thinking how much Grace resembled her mother. He pulled over, got out and walked toward the driveway. "Hello Mrs. Devlin. It's Aidan McRae. Remember me?"

She raised a hand to shield her eyes before answering. "Aidan, of course. I couldn't see you. The sun was in my eyes. Are you just getting into town?"

"Yes. I'm on my way to my dad's."

She popped open her trunk. "I'd love to talk, but I have to get this food in the house."

He went to the back of her car. "Let me help you."

Some of the bags were heavy. She wasn't about to turn down his offer. "Thank you. I've been shopping for the cookout."

After all the groceries were in the kitchen, he started emptying the bags. "You don't have to do that. Getting it all in here was a big help."

"I don't mind. I'm used to it."

He was more handsome than she remembered. *No wonder Grace looked so happy when she came home from Maine.* "Do you have time for a glass of lemonade?"

"Thanks, Mrs. Devlin, but my dad's expecting me. By the way, I want to thank you for inviting him to the cookout. He's looking forward to it."

"I'm glad he could come. And, call me Janet. Mrs. Devlin makes me feel old. I'm sure I'll see you before then. Grace will probably send you and Jimmy after my folding table. Thanks again for your help. Say hello to Donald for me."

When Aidan pulled up in front of the old house on Carlton Road, his dad was on the front porch watering the flowers. He got his suitcase out of the truck and headed up the walkway.

"Hi, Dad. Flowers look good."

"Mornin' son. Startin' to get a little worried. Traffic heavy?"

"Sorry. I took the scenic route through town."

"I thought maybe you stopped off to see Grace first."

"No, but I did help her mother carry in groceries."

Donald put the watering can down and turned toward his son. Janet's place is clear across town. "You did take the scenic route."

"Just drove around a little. Went by the high school and a couple places. I happened to go by as she was getting out of her car. I stopped to say hi and helped her with the bundles. She said to say hello."

"That's nice."

"Grace reminded me you two are on some committees together."

He held the screen door open for Aidan. "We both do volunteer work."

Aidan had a feeling he was leaving something out, but didn't dare suggest it. "I'll put my suitcase upstairs and come back down for my tools. I brought wood to fix the step."

"Take your time. I picked up some groceries. Figured you'd be hungry after the long ride."

"Great."

Aidan called Grace from his room. "I'm at my dad's."

"So I heard."

"I take it you talked to your mom."

Grace laughed. "Of course. She told me your timing was perfect."

"I just happened to be going by."

"She really appreciated it. I'll see you later today or tonight, right?"

"Absolutely. I'm gonna spend some time with my dad and fix the back step this afternoon. What's your schedule look like?"

"The house is clean. Jimmy's taking care of the pool. I have to do the grocery shopping. Nothing else for tonight. Tomorrow will be busy."

"I'll text you when I'm about done here. Maybe we could go for a walk on the beach and grab a bite to eat."

"Sounds wonderful. I can't wait to see you. I'm so happy you're here."

"Me too."

⸻

Donald helped Aidan carry his tools to the back yard. "I got the steak tips you wanted for the cookout. I'm making my famous marinated mushrooms."

Aidan teased his dad. "I knew they were good. Had no idea they were famous."

"Around here they are. People always ask me to make my famous mushrooms when they invite me to a party."

"Oh?" Aidan put his tools down and turned toward his dad. "Did someone ask you to make them for the cookout?"

"No, but Janet likes them. Been after my recipe for years."

Aidan caught the hint of a smile when his father mentioned Grace's mom. *Am I missing something here?*

"Come on in and have a sandwich before you start workin' on that step."

Aidan followed his dad into the kitchen. He pictured his mother at the sink washing dishes, or standing in front of the stove. If he closed his eyes, he could smell the peanut butter cookies or the chocolate cake she had waiting for him after school. No wonder his father never wanted to remodel it.

They took their time over lunch. "If there's anything else you need me to fix while I'm here, let me know."

"The step's enough. I know you'll want to spend time with Grace alone before all the hoopla begins."

"I would like to take her out for dinner."

"Black Rock Tavern on the beach is supposed to be nice. Opened up in the spring."

"Have you been there?"

"Not for dinner. Been wanting to try it though."

"Why haven't you?"

"Haven't been able to get up the nerve to ask her to go with me."

Aidan put his sandwich down and reached for his water. "Who?"

"Janet, of course."

Aidan was glad he wasn't chewing. He might have choked. "Mrs. Devlin? Grace's mom?"

"She's a good lookin' woman, don't ya think? Pretty auburn hair. Nice too."

Aidan didn't understand. "Dad, you're not exactly teenagers. If you're interested in Janet, why don't you ask her out?"

Donald looked down at the table then back up at his son. "To tell you the truth, I thought about it several times over the past few years. Gave her a ride home one night from a meeting. I came close to asking her, but thought better of it."

"What made you change your mind?"

"To be honest, it was Grace."

"Grace. What does Grace have to do with it?"

"I didn't know how she'd feel about her mother going out with me."

Aidan was beginning to get the picture. "You mean because of me."

"I was afraid I'd remind her too much of the past."

"Dad, I'm sorry. But, things have changed now. I don't think Grace would mind at all. It was her mother who invited you to the big hoopla. Maybe she's waiting for you to make a move."

"We'll see, son. We'll see. Now, let's get that step fixed so you don't keep the lady waiting."

Aidan fixed the step and helped his dad with some boxes he wanted to store in the basement. Donald appreciated the help, but he didn't want his son to spend most of his visit fixing things. He wanted to have quality time with him.

"That's enough work. How 'bout coffee and a piece of apple pie? It's still early enough not to spoil your appetite for dinner. We can catch up some more."

"Sounds good to me. You put the coffee on. I'll get the cups and give Grace a quick call."

"Hi. Thought I'd call instead of texting."

"It's nice to hear your voice. How are things going at your dad's?"

"Good. We're about to have coffee and catch up. How are things going with you?"

"Great. Shopping's done. I was about to get in the shower. What time do you want to pick me up?"

He didn't answer right away. "Is something wrong?"

"No. It just seems so strange to be able to pick you up at your house."

Grace knew exactly what he meant. "It felt strange to say it."

"How's five sound? I was thinking we could take a walk on the beach and then grab a bite at the Black Rock."

"Perfect. I'm looking forward to some time alone with you. There'll be a lot of people around the rest of the weekend."

"I know. My dad's excited about being invited. Will your kids be home today?"

"I'm not sure, but don't worry about it. Jimmy's looking forward to meeting you."

"I guess one out of two ain't bad. See you at five."

Aidan got two mugs and a couple of small plates out of the cabinet and placed them on the table.

"The pie looks good."

Donald poured the coffee. "It is. Got it at Mia's. Fresh baked this morning. Let's have it outside."

Aidan cut them each a slice and followed his dad out to the front porch.

"You're right. This is good."

"Not as good as your mother's, but it's good."

The two men sat for an hour catching up. Donald filled his son in on the local gossip. Most of it meant nothing to Aidan, but he knew his dad was enjoying the company. He was too.

Donald finished his coffee and put the cup down. "I miss sittin' out here with her. We'd come out and talk about the day or local gossip. Sometimes, we didn't talk. Didn't need to. Just sat. When you can do that with a woman, you know you got somethin' special."

Aidan understood exactly. "I know what you mean, Dad."

CHAPTER 52
AIDAN MEETS THE KIDS

There was a black Toyota parked in Grace's driveway when Aidan arrived. His mouth went a little dry. *This is ridiculous. I have to meet her kids some time. Wish I wasn't so nervous.* He parked the truck and headed up the walkway.

Hoping Grace would answer, he rang the bell. "I'll get it!" Someone inside yelled.

Aidan was relieved it was Jimmy and not Elise who opened the door. "Hi. I'm Aidan McRae. I'm here to see Grace."

The young man smiled and opened the door further. "Come in, Mr. McRae. My mother's expecting you. I'm Jim."

Aidan held out his hand. "Nice to meet you, Jim. Your mom's told me a lot about you. And, please, call me Aidan."

Jimmy shook his hand. He liked that he didn't call him Jimmy. "I've heard a lot about you as well. It's good to meet you, too."

"Mum, Aidan's here!" Jimmy announced, loudly.

"I'll be right down!"

"Let's go in the living room. She won't be long."
Aidan followed him. "Thanks."
"Can I get you anything?"
"No, thank you. I'm all set."
"Mum tells me you own a hardware store."
"That's right. I hear you're going to law school."
"Yeah. Did she tell you I know your dad? I've met your daughter too."
"Yes, she did. My dad says you do good work."
Jimmy felt his face turning red. "I like your dad. He's a good guy. I hear your daughter is in real estate."
Aidan was about to answer when he heard car doors slamming and voices coming from outside.
"Sounds like my sister and Brian."
"Is Brian her boyfriend?"
"Sort of. I know you're probably worried about meeting Elise. Don't let her get to you. She's really not a bad person. I'm sure she'll be okay with things once she gets to know you."
Aidan was glad he had Jimmy on his side. "Thanks for the vote of confidence."
Elise saw Aidan's truck out front. "Looks like lover boy's here."
"At least give the guy a chance, Elise. You don't even know him yet. Your mom's not stupid. He must be a decent guy or she wouldn't be going out with him."
Elise shot Brian a look, but refrained from telling him what she was thinking. "Let's get this over with."
Elise walked into the living room with Brian behind her. "I see we have company."

Aidan stood up. Elise looked like Grace when she was younger. Her hair was a darker red, but the green eyes that glared at him were her mother's.

Jimmy stood up and turned toward his sister. "Elise, this is Aidan McRae. Aidan, this is my sister, Elise and her friend Brian O'Leary."

Aidan wished Grace would hurry up and get downstairs. "It's nice to meet you."

When he held his hand out, Elise ignored it. Brian tried to cover up the awkward moment by stepping in front of her and shaking Aidan's hand.

"Nice to meet you, Mr. McRae."

Brian reminded Aidan a little of Todd. "Please, call me Aidan."

Elise was still sizing him up. *He is kind of cute, for an older guy. I guess I can see how she'd be attracted to him. Jimmy's sucking up to him. This is going to be some 4th of July.* Knowing she'd never hear the end of it if she were rude to him, Elise finally spoke.

"So, we finally get to meet mom's mystery man."

Aidan couldn't help but smile. "A little reserved maybe, but hardly a mystery."

"What I meant was, we've heard very little about you. My mother has managed to keep you a secret until she went to Maine for a book signing."

Aidan knew what she was getting at. "It's no secret your mom and I dated when we were in college. Things didn't work out between us. I moved to Maine after I got out of the service. I heard she was coming to my friend's bookstore and went to see her. We hadn't seen each other in over twenty-four years."

Elise might have thought it was a romantic story if he was talking about someone other than her mother. *He knows what I'm trying to find out. He's pretty smart. But, I don't trust him.*

Jimmy wanted to grab his sister and shake her. *What is she trying to imply?* "Why don't we all sit down? My mother should be ready shortly."

Brian sat in the chair facing Aidan. "So, you're from Maine. My parents have a small house in Wells. They vacation there and go up on weekends a lot."

"Wells is a nice area. I live in Casselton. Not that far from it."

Elise wasn't happy with Brian at the moment. *Great. They're bonding. Whose side is he on?* "Mom says you have a daughter."

Aidan was feeling more comfortable. At least Elise was talking. "Yes. Kelli's twenty-three. She lives in Bridgeton."

He was glad to see Grace coming down the stairs. "I'm sorry I kept you waiting. My publisher called and I couldn't get him off the phone. I see you've all met."

Aidan stood again when she came into the room. She walked over to him and gave him a quick hug. "It's good to see you. Everything go well at your dad's today?"

"Yes. He was happy to get the step fixed. He said to tell you he has some folding chairs you can borrow if you need them."

"I might take him up on that. Jimmy can go with you tomorrow to help. I was going to send the two of you to my mom's to pick up her table."

Brian chimed in again. "I'm available to help with the set up too, Mrs. Madden."

"Thanks, Brian. Well, shall we go? I'm getting hungry."

Before he followed Grace out, Aidan said his good-byes. "Night Jim, Brian. See you both tomorrow." He looked at Elise. She wasn't glaring as much as when he first met her, but she wasn't smiling either. "Good night, Elise. It was nice meeting you."

Grace turned before opening the door to leave. "We're going to the Black Rock for dinner. See you all later."

When they got in Aidan's truck, she leaned over and kissed his cheek. "I'm sorry. I was ready, but I waited to come down when I heard Elise. You were doing so well on your own, I didn't want to interrupt."

"Gee thanks. A few more minutes and we'd have been best friends, I'm sure." He laughed. "Seriously, I was scared to death. She's tough."

CHAPTER 53
ELISE, BRIAN AND JIMMY

Elise stood in the living room expecting Jimmy to give her a hard time about the way she behaved. Brian's reaction surprised her.

"I hope you're proud of yourself."

"I just asked him a few questions. What's your problem?"

"You were rude and sarcastic. Do you think he didn't know what you were implying?"

Jimmy jumped in. "Come on, Elise. You insinuated he had something going with Mum way before her trip to Maine."

"You don't know that he didn't."

Jimmy couldn't take much more of his sister's accusations. "I know my mother! You're suggesting she cheated on Dad. What the hell is wrong with you? You should be ashamed of yourself for thinking such a thing."

Brian agreed with Jimmy. "Elise, your brother's right."

She turned and took a step toward Brian. "So you're taking his side?"

"I'm not taking anyone's side. I'm saying you're wrong. Listen to yourself. You can't honestly believe your mother would do something like that."

"You didn't read her book."

"I didn't have to. Besides, it's fiction."

"It's about them!"

Brian threw his hands up in the air and began shouting. "Elise, I don't know what's going on with you lately, but I've had about all I can take! You used to be a sweet, thoughtful girl."

Elise had never seen Brian this angry.

He lowered his voice and continued. "After your dad died, you went through a tough time. I understood. I tried to be there for you. You pushed me away. I figured you needed to sort things out, so I left you alone. Then, for a while, you seemed like your old self. I thought we were getting closer. I thought this was becoming a serious thing between us."

"Now you're obsessed with this crazy idea about your mom. It's destroying your relationship with her and it's destroying us. I can't be serious about a woman who would disrespect her own mother and begrudge her the happiness she deserves. I want that sweet, thoughtful girl back."

He waited for a response from Elise. When he didn't get one, Brian turned toward Jimmy. "I'll be around tomorrow to help set up for the cookout like I promised."

He turned back toward Elise as he headed for the door. "I'm not sure about the fireworks."

When the door closed behind Brian, Jimmy looked at his sister. "I hope you're satisfied."

CHAPTER 54
DINNER AT THE BLACK ROCK

Aidan parked along the beach, not far from the Black Rock Tavern. He was happy to be alone with Grace before the festivities of the next couple of days began. "Want to eat first and then go for a walk on the beach?"

"That sounds great. We can watch the sunset."

The restaurant wasn't crowded yet. They were able to get a table by the huge wall of windows. Aidan noticed the woodworking on the long bar near the entrance. A round bar, further into the dining area, was a perfect spot to have a drink and look out at the Atlantic. The layout of the entire room was about the view.

Aidan was impressed. "I like what they've done with this place. You can see Boston from here."

"Yes, it's lovely. I like the high ceilings and the spectacular ocean views from just about anywhere you sit."

"I could use a beer after that meeting. How about you?"

Grace smiled at him. "At least the initial meeting is over. You did great. You can relax now. I could use a glass of white wine. But, only one. Tomorrow's going to be busy."

They ordered their drinks and watched the early evening activity on the beach. Couples walked along the water's edge. Children built sandcastles while their mothers sat nearby reading or playing with their phones.

"I took a ride by here this morning when I got into town. I'd forgotten how beautiful the ocean is. I love living on the lake, but I miss the smell of the salty air and seeing the waves. This is the first time I've come home that I ventured past my dad's house."

"Coming home was that difficult for you?"

"Yes. Visiting was hard. I always pictured running into you when I went to the store for a newspaper or passing you in traffic. One time, a couple of years ago, I drove by your house and stopped across the street for a few minutes. You came out of the house and got in your car. I buried my face in a road map so you wouldn't notice me. I felt like a stalker and never did it again."

Grace felt sad that he had to go through that. "I had no idea."

"How could you?"

They talked a bit more about his meeting the kids and the plans for the rest of the weekend. Part of the time, they sat silently, just enjoying the view and being together. Aidan thought about what his dad said earlier. He knew they had something special.

After dinner, they walked along the boulevard. Aidan wrapped his arm around her shoulder. A warm breeze blew her hair against his cheek. He reached over, brushed it away and kissed her.

She thought about the cars driving by and who might see them. What if her kids rode by? "Why don't we walk down on the beach? It'll be more private."

The traffic was making him self-conscious too. No telling who might see them. It made it hard to steal a kiss. "Good idea."

He led her down the stairs to the beach. They slipped their sandals off when they got to the last step. The sand felt cool on their bare feet. The children were gone now, leaving their sandcastles to wash away with the incoming tide.

Aidan took her hand. They walked toward the foamy waves, jumping back quickly and laughing as the icy water hit their toes. "I haven't done this in years."

She pointed to a large boat off in the distance. "Every so often we see a cruise ship coming out of Boston."

"There's something you don't see on a lake."

"You don't see the Boston skyline either. Remember how pretty it looks at night?"

"Not really. I was always looking at you."

"Well look at it tonight. It's very romantic."

Aidan cleared his throat. "Speaking of romantic…how am I going to be near you for the next two days and not be able to make love to you?"

"It won't be easy for me either. But, we can't stay holed up in Maine all the time, you know. We won't have the privacy here we're used to."

Sliding one arm around her waist, he moved her away from the water and pulled her close to him. "Then let's make good use of our time right now."

Far enough away from the traffic to lose all inhibitions, he kissed her the way he'd been wanting to all evening.

They walked a little further, stopping now and then to pick up a pretty shell. He took pictures of her with his phone. "I wish I'd thought to bring a blanket."

Grace laughed at the image that came to her. "That's okay. Better that we're standing."

Aidan led her to the last staircase. They put their shoes on, climbed back up to the sidewalk and headed for the park that overlooks the rocky area below. "We can sit over there on one of the benches and watch the sunset."

They sat listening to the waves breaking against the rocks below. A bright yellow glow streaked the buildings in Boston. Resting her head on Aidan's shoulder, Grace leaned into him. "Remember climbing out onto the rocks when we were kids?"

He remembered how nothing frightened them then. "I like my comfort now."

"Me too."

Together, they watched the deep yellow ball sink into the horizon, like they did before life got complicated.

CHAPTER 55
AT THE CEMETERY

Aidan poured himself a cup of coffee and joined Donald on the front porch. "Morning, Dad."

His father looked over the top of his newspaper. "Didn't expect to see you up so early. How was your date with Grace?"

"Great. Thanks for the tip on the restaurant. You should try it."

Aidan noticed the hint of a smile on his father's face as he handed him the comic section of the Globe. "Might just do that."

They sat reading until Aidan got hungry. "How 'bout I make some breakfast?"

"Good idea. I like my eggs…"

Aidan interrupted him. "I know. Over easy, bacon crisp."

After they ate, the two men had a second cup of coffee. "What time's Grace expecting you this morning?"

"Around eleven, I think. I'll call her in a while. I want to go by the cemetery and visit Mom first."

"Did you tell Grace about the folding chairs?"

"I did. Are you going to the fireworks with us tonight, or meeting us there?"

Donald hesitated before he answered. "Check with me later."

After they cleaned up the kitchen, Aidan put the folding chairs in the back of his truck and called Grace.

"Good morning. Sleep well?"

"Pretty well, considering I was alone. How about you?"

"A cold shower when I got home helped."

"I'm sorry we won't have any alone time this weekend."

"It's okay. At least we're together. What time do you want me there today?"

"Between eleven and noon would be great. I'll have you and Jonathan set up the yard. Jimmy and Brian will fill the coolers. Charlene can help in the kitchen."

"How's Elise this morning?"

"She's in a snit. She had an argument with Brian yesterday."

"Brian seems like he can handle her. Other than that, you seem to have things under control. The chairs are in my truck. I'll bring the steak tips tomorrow. Anything else you need?"

"I don't think so. Is your dad coming to the fireworks with us?"

"I'm not sure. He was a bit vague when I asked. Maybe he'll meet us there. I need to do a couple of errands first and visit my mom."

Grace understood. "See you when you get here."

On the way to Elmwood Cemetery, he stopped at the supermarket and bought a single red rose.

Aidan hated cemeteries. Seeing the tiny flags in the section singled out for veterans brought back painful memories.

It made him think about the friends he lost and the men and women who didn't make it home.

He drove around to the older, more secluded section where Emma McRae was buried and parked his truck. He didn't notice the car, a little further down, or the young red-haired girl near it. Holding the rose, Aidan walked toward the black and silver granite stone with his mother's name on it. He knelt down, placed the rose in front of it and started to pray.

A woman screaming interrupted his prayers. "Hey, get out of here! What do you think you're doing! Come back here with my purse you scumbag!"

Aidan stood up. He saw a young girl on the ground. A male figure with a large pink handbag under his arm was running away. He ran toward the girl, not realizing who she was until he got to her. "Elise!"

She was just as surprised to see him. "Aidan! What are you doing here?"

"Never mind that. Are you hurt?"

"I'm okay. He took my purse."

"Get in your car. Lock it and call 9-1-1."

Elise did what he told her. Horrified, she watched the man she had been so mean to run after the despicable person who stole her pocketbook while she was visiting her grandfather's grave.

The guy had a good head start, but Aidan knew his way around the cemetery. He weaved around headstones, closing the gap a little. The assailant looked back and saw he was being chased. He threw the bag on the ground. Just when Aidan was about to give up, the guy headed toward a path that led to a dead end. To get out, he'd have to climb a high fence. *Gotcha now. You've got nowhere to go.*

Aidan got to him as he was trying to scale the fence. He grabbed the back of his shirt, pulled him off the fence, knocked him down and held him on the ground.

The kid appeared to be in his late teens. "Let go of me! I dropped the bag." He swung at Aidan.

Aidan pinned his arms down and kept one knee on his chest. It took a considerable amount of restraint not to punch the guy. "Keep moving and I'll squash you like a bug."

"Okay! Okay!"

Elise pulled up beside them, slammed on the brakes and jumped out of the car. "The police are on their way. Are you okay, Aidan?"

He hadn't run like that in a long time. His hand hurt and he was short of breath. "Yeah." He let out a breath. "I'm okay. Get back in the car."

She ignored his order. "Brian and Jimmy are on their way here too."

Aidan thought of Grace. "You didn't call your mother, did you?"

"No."

"Good. Let's get you home first."

They heard the sirens. Within seconds, a police cruiser, an ambulance and a fire engine were there. Two officers got out and hurried over to help Aidan. They stood the kid up and handcuffed him. One of them turned toward Elise.

"Are you hurt, Miss?"

Elise was crying. "No. I'm okay."

Aidan wasn't so sure. "Would it be all right if she sits in her car until you're ready to talk to us? Her brother and boyfriend are on their way here."

"Sure. We'll get our friend here settled and then we'd like to ask both of you some questions. This is the fourth time in the last three weeks this has happened in two different cemeteries. We've been lookin' for this kid."

Aidan helped Elise into her car. "It's okay. It's over. Take a few deep breaths. When Brian gets here, I'll get your purse."

Elise tried to tell him what happened. "I didn't see him coming. I heard a noise. When I turned around, he was grabbing my purse off the front seat. I ran around to the front of the car and tried to stop him. I don't know why I did that. He pushed me down. I started screaming at him."

Those green eyes were so much like her mother's. Aidan hated to see them clouded with tears. He knew she shouldn't have tried to stop the guy, but he couldn't stifle a smile. "You sure did. Are you positive you're not hurt?"

"Just a few scrapes. No big deal."

The EMT's came over to Aidan. "Are either of you in need of medical attention?"

He tried again. "Why don't you have the paramedics take a look at those scrapes and clean them up a little?"

"Okay, but I think you should do the same."

"What?" He'd been too concerned about Elise to give any thought to the bruise on his hand.

"Why don't we take a look at both of you?"

Brian and Jimmy showed up as the fire engine was pulling away. A second cruiser had just arrived. The paramedics were assisting Elise and Aidan. The two young men jumped out of Brian's pick-up and hurried over to her car.

Brian went straight to Elise. "Are you okay? What happened?"

She started to cry again. "Just some scrapes, but I'm fine, really." Brian put both arms around her.

Jimmy thought about how angry he had been at his sister earlier. *What if something worse had happened to her?* "Thank God you're both all right. Does Mum know?"

Aidan spoke up. "No. We still have to talk to the police. I thought it best if you bring your sister home and tell her then. That way, she can see Elise is okay."

"What about you?"

"I'll go home, clean up and come over later."

"Aidan, will you call Mom? She's going to be angry at me for being in that part of the cemetery alone."

Her request surprised him. "I will if you want me to, but I'm sure she'll be too thankful you're unharmed to be angry. Parents are funny like that."

Aidan looked at Jimmy and Brian. "You two stay with Elise. I'll go get my truck and see if I can find her purse. He dropped it over there somewhere. After we give our statements to the police, I'll call your mother."

Jimmy wanted to talk to Aidan alone. "Brian, you stay with Elise? I'll go with Aidan."

They found the bag and headed for Aidan's truck. "Can you give me a minute, Jim? I was in the middle of something when this all started."

Jimmy waited for Aidan in his truck.

"I can't thank you enough. I don't even want to think about what might have happened if it hadn't been for you. What you did was dangerous. He might have had a weapon."

"Just a gut reaction, I guess."

When they got back, the police had taken the kid away. The two officers who were first on the scene took their statements and told them they were free to go. One officer turned to Aidan. "Thank you, Mr. McRae. We've been after this kid for three weeks."

Jimmy turned to Aidan. "We'll get my sister and her car home."

"I'll call your mother and let her know."

As soon as they left, Aidan pulled out his phone and called Grace.

CHAPTER 56
GRACE FINDS OUT

Grace was in the kitchen with Valerie when the phone rang. "I hope that's Aidan. I don't know what's keeping him."

"Hi Honey, it's me."

"Where are you? I was beginning to worry."

He figured it was best to just come out and tell her. "I've been detained. Is Jonathan there yet?"

Grace could tell by his voice something was wrong. "No. Valerie's here though. What do you mean detained?"

He was glad she wasn't alone. "Grace, there was an incident at the cemetery."

She felt a flutter in her stomach. "You mean an accident? Are you all right?"

"I'm fine. Everyone is fine. It wasn't an accident. I saw a guy steal a purse out of a young girl's car while visiting my mother's grave."

"Oh?"

"Grace, it was Elise. She's okay. She's not hurt. Brian and Jimmy are bringing her home right now."

"Elise! Oh my God! I don't understand." She had to sit down.

Valerie hurried to her side. "What's wrong?"

She turned to tell her friend. "Elise's purse was stolen out of her car at the cemetery. Aidan was there. He witnessed it."

"Aidan, what happened? Are you sure she's all right?"

"She's got a few scrapes. She's scared and pretty shaken, but okay. We had to stay and talk to the police."

Grace was afraid he was not telling her the whole story. "The police? Just how involved were you? Why aren't you coming here now? Were you hurt?"

"One question at a time, Gracie. I'm not hurt. I thought you might want some time alone with Elise. I'm going home to clean up and change. I'll be there as soon as I can."

"Wait. Why do you have to clean up?"

He knew the kids would tell her anyway. "I chased the guy and caught up with him. There was a bit of a scuffle. I'm fine. The police now have him in custody. Try to stay calm. Elise is afraid you're going to be angry with her."

"Angry? Why?"

"Something about being in that part of the cemetery alone."

"I'm not angry. I'm happy she wasn't seriously hurt. I won't be all right until I know for sure you weren't hurt either, so get here as soon as you can."

"I will. And, Gracie…I love you."

"I love you, too."

Grace fought back tears. Valerie got her a glass of water. "You have to be strong. You can't let her see you fall apart."

"I'll be okay. What if Aidan hadn't been there, Val?"

They heard cars pull into the driveway. Grace pulled herself together and waited for them.

Jimmy could tell by the look on his mother's face she had spoken to Aidan. "She's okay, Mum. Aidan's okay too."

Brian and Elise were right behind him. "Hi, Mrs. Madden."

Grace saw the bandages on Elise's arms and could tell she'd been crying, but other than a tear in her jeans, she looked fine. "Thank you for bringing her home."

Elise looked at Grace. "Are you mad at me?"

With her arms held out, Grace moved toward her daughter. "Of course not. I'm thankful you're all right. When I think what could have happened."

She hugged Elise. "Does it hurt when I hug you?"

"A hug never hurts."

In the comfort of her mother's arms, Elise felt safe again.

After a few minutes, Grace pulled back and looked her over. "Are you sure you're not hurt anywhere else?"

"I'm sure. Aidan hurt his hand though. You should have seen him go after the guy. That boyfriend of yours can run."

"What happened to his hand?"

"Didn't he tell you? He's okay. They cleaned it up and bandaged it."

"He mentioned a scuffle."

"Scuffle? Is that what he called it? He tackled the guy, knocked him to the ground and held him there until the police came."

Grace wanted to see Aidan. She needed to see for herself he was unharmed. First, she had to take care of her daughter. "Are you hungry?"

"A little. I'm more tired than anything else."

"I'll make you a sandwich and a cup of tea. Then, you can go upstairs and take a nice nap."

"But, I want to help you get ready for tomorrow."

"You can help later. We've got plenty of men for the heavy stuff. Jonathan's bringing Charlene. She can help with the food. Valerie's here already and Gran's coming. There'll be plenty for you to do tomorrow when you're feeling better."

For once, Elise didn't argue. All she wanted was to go to sleep and forget about this whole morning.

CHAPTER 57
PREPARING FOR THE COOKOUT

Grace got Elise settled in her room. When she came downstairs, Janet was in the kitchen.
"How's Elise?"
"She's resting, but how did you know?"
"Donald called me."
"Of course, Aidan would have told his dad."
"No. One of the officers is a friend of Donald's. He recognized the name and called him."
"Aidan should be here any minute. I still haven't heard the whole story. I'd appreciate it if you could keep things going in the kitchen when he gets here so I can talk to him privately for a few minutes."
"No problem. How's the set-up going so far?"
"We're a bit off schedule, but we'll make it. Jimmy and Brian went to get gas for the grills. I'll send them after a couple of coolers. I have one big one. They can pick up the

ice in the morning. Aidan's bringing more folding chairs. Once they're all here, they can set up the tables and chairs."

"Sounds like you've got a good handle on things. Try to relax before the fireworks."

"I will."

A truck pulled into the driveway. "That must be Aidan."

He went around to the back. Grace was already waiting at the door. A giant bandage covered most of the back of his left hand. "I'm so glad you're finally here. Come on in."

"Sorry it took me so long. Dad had to hear the whole story and I was hungry so I had lunch with him. How's Elise?"

"She was tired. She's resting now. What about you? Why didn't you tell me about your hand?"

"It wasn't that big a deal. I had to tell you what happened before the kids got home."

Janet stepped into the kitchen. "Hello, Aidan. We're all so grateful you were there this morning. I'm glad you weren't badly injured. Grace, why don't you and Aidan go into the den and talk? I know you want to hear the whole story."

"Thanks, Mom."

Aidan followed her into the den. She closed the door and wrapped her arms around his waist, resting her head on his chest. "I've been so worried."

"I told you I was fine."

"I know, but I needed to see for myself."

"I'm sorry. I didn't want you to worry. You have enough going on with Elise."

"I keep thinking what might have happened if you hadn't been there."

"I don't think he was out to hurt anyone. This sort of thing is usually someone looking for quick cash. They look for a woman alone. If she's not holding a purse, it's a good guess she left it on the front seat. They sneak up, grab the bag and run. They usually take the money out and drop the bag somewhere."

Grace leaned back and looked up at him. "But, Jimmy said he knocked her down."

Aidan stifled a laugh. "That's because that little spitfire of yours tried to stop him."

"She what? They left that part out."

"I think she just reacted. She knows it wasn't the right thing to do."

"So, if you were nearby, she must have been visiting her grandfather. He's in the older section where your mother is. I've told her so many times not to go there alone. It's too secluded. How ironic that you should be there."

"I heard a woman screaming. I had no idea it was Elise until I got to her. She said he stole her purse. I told her to lock herself in her car and call 9-1-1. He dropped the bag when he realized he was being chased. Probably thought I'd stop. I might not have caught him if he hadn't gone down a path with no way out."

"Aidan, I don't know what to say. I'm so blown away by all of this."

He smiled at her. "How about less talk and more action before we have to go back and get some work done?"

When he kissed her, she blocked out all the voices and noise coming from the kitchen.

Aidan pulled away. "I guess we'd better get out there before I have to go home and take another cold shower."

"I guess you're right. I think Jonathan and Charlene are here."

There was a lot of commotion in the kitchen. Jonathan was introducing Charlene. When Grace and Aidan walked in, everyone stopped talking.

Aidan looked around the room. "We could go back out if you want."

They all laughed. Jonathan stepped forward and extended his hand. "Aidan. Good to see you. You know Charlene."

"Of course." He shook Jonathan's hand and gave Charlene a hug and a kiss on the cheek. "Nice to see both of you. Glad you could make it, Charlene. You know Grace."

Grace hugged Charlene. "I'm glad you are here. Have you met everyone?"

"Yes. Thank you so much for inviting me. You have a lovely home."

"Thank you."

Grace reached out for Jonathan. "I'm happy you're here."

He hugged her and kissed her cheek. "I'm happy to be here. How's Elise."

"She's resting. It was a harrowing experience for her. How did you find out?"

"It was on the radio. Apparently, it was an experience for you too, Aidan. I don't think I could have done what you did."

Grace sensed Aidan's nervousness. She drew the attention away from him. "I think we need to get things set up or we'll miss the fireworks tonight."

Jonathan stepped up. "Okay, Boss Lady. Tell us what you need done."

Grace gave everyone assignments. "Jonathan, I'll need you and Brian here to start setting up the tables and chairs. Jimmy and Brian can help Aidan get the extra chairs out of his truck."

"Then, Aidan, you go with Jimmy to pick up the coolers. He knows who has the ones we're borrowing. The grills are all set and ready. Jimmy, did you and Brian put the extra can of gas in the shed?"

"Yes, Mum."

"Great. Val, you make the pasta salad. Charlene can wash the lettuce and tomatoes for the garden salad. Elise will put it together in the morning. Once the tables are set up, Charlene and Val, the plastic tablecloths are in the box with the utensils and napkins. Aidan and I will shuck the corn and wrap it in foil. When we're done, I'll order pizza. Then I think we should relax and get ready for the fireworks. Mom, are you staying or going home to rest for a while?"

Grace thought her mother looked a little flush. "Mom, is anything wrong?"

"No. I was just thinking about something. I'm going home to make the potato salad.

"Are you coming back to go to the fireworks with us, or meeting us there?"

Janet got up to leave. "We'll see you there."

"We'll?"

Janet seemed flustered. "I meant WILL see you there. I know where to find you."

"Okay."

Janet rushed out the back door and hurried to her car. *I can't believe I said that. Leave it to Grace to pick up on it.*

Grace looked at Aidan. "That was strange."

"Funny, my dad was acting weird about the fireworks, now that you mention it. He said he'll meet us there, too. Did I tell you he's making his marinated mushrooms? He said your mom likes them."

"Really? How sweet."

"I guess she's been after him for the recipe."

"My mom knew about what happened today before I did. She said your dad called her even before you went home and told him."

"One of the cops called him. He didn't tell me he called your mom, though."

Aidan scratched his head. "If you ask me, somethin's going on with those two."

Grace shrugged it off. "Well, I'm sure we'll find out soon enough. Let's get to work."

CHAPTER 58
FIREWORKS

By six o'clock, the tables and chairs were in place, grills were ready and the coolers were waiting for ice. Vegetables were washed. A pasta salad was chilling. The corn was wrapped in foil and being kept in the spare fridge in the garage. Grace ordered pizza for everyone. They ate by the pool and relaxed until it was time to go to the fireworks.

Elise got up and went inside. Jonathan followed her. He found her in the den sitting in her dad's recliner. "I thought I'd find you in here. Everything okay?"

"Yeah, I'm still a little tired. I keep seeing that guy grabbing my purse off the seat of my car and Aidan chasing after him. I can't get the images out of my head."

"It'll take a while. But, you're safe. Aidan's safe. You got your purse back." He looked at the bandages on her arms and couldn't help thinking how much worse it could have been. "You were very lucky."

"I know. I can't believe I was stupid enough to try to stop the creep. I keep thinking what might have happened if Aidan hadn't been there, or if the guy had a gun. Aidan took an awful chance."

"Yes, he did. He's not such a bad guy after all. Guess you and I should have trusted your mother's instincts. We'd have saved ourselves a lot of grief."

She smiled for the first time all day. "Ya think? I'm lucky for a lot of other reasons too."

"You have a lot of people who love you, Elise."

"I know. And I don't want to disappoint them anymore. I almost lost Brian. Still might."

"Oh, I don't think Brian's going anywhere. He was pretty upset today."

"I told him I don't want to go to the fireworks tonight and he understood. He said he'd stay home with me."

"How come you don't want to go?"

"The story's all over town. My phone's been ringing like crazy. I don't feel up to answering questions and reliving it tonight. Do you think my mother will be disappointed if I don't go?"

"Not at all. She'll understand. Why don't you come back outside now? I'll tell her if you want me to."

"Thanks. By the way, Charlene's very nice."

"Come on out and get to know her a little better. She likes you too."

Happy to see her smiling again, he led her out to the yard.

Grace noticed Elise and Jonathan coming out of the house. *I hope she's all right. She still looks tired. She should stay home tonight, but I don't dare suggest it.*

Aidan saw them too. He also saw Grace's look of concern. "She'll be fine. She has to work it out for herself."

"I know. Thanks for reminding me, though."

"Come on. I'll help you get rid of these pizza boxes and clean up."

When they were done, Aidan cornered her in the kitchen and tried to steal a kiss.

Jonathan and Charlene walked in on them. "Looks like this room's taken. Want to go out to my car?"

Charlene knew he was joking, but she was embarrassed about walking in on Grace and Aidan.

Aidan, like Jonathan, tried to lessen the awkward feeling. "It's pretty pathetic when we have to sneak around just to get a kiss."

Grace sensed Charlene's discomfort. "Stop it you two. Charlene won't want to come back."

Jonathan put his arm around her waist. "I'll have to make it worth her while."

Charlene appreciated Grace's effort to make her feel at home. "What time do we leave for the fireworks?"

"We'll start rounding them up and deciding who is going in whose car or truck. The less vehicles, the better."

Aidan looked at Jonathan. "The four of us can go together in my truck."

Jonathan agreed. "Sounds good to me."

"Jimmy will be going with his friends. Elise and Brian can go in his truck."

Jonathan interrupted. "Grace. I talked to Elise earlier. She's not up to the fireworks tonight. She wants to stay home with Brian. She's afraid to tell you."

"Fine with me. I don't think she should go anyway."

Aidan looked at Grace. "In that case, Val can come with us in my truck and we'll only have one vehicle to park."

They got everyone together and headed for the beach. Aidan parked a few streets over. The five of them got out and walked from there. "I hope your mom and my dad can find us. I told him where we'd be."

"My mom knows where we stand every year. She'll find us."

They walked to their usual viewing spot. Grace looked around. She didn't see her mother anywhere. "I'll text her if she doesn't show up soon."

"I don't see my dad either. He may have decided not to come."

Grace was glad Elise decided to stay home. Just about every person they ran into asked about the incident. Everyone wanted a detailed accounting of what happened and they all wanted to meet Aidan, if they didn't already know him. She tried to keep it short with all of them by saying the fireworks were about to start.

Jimmy and a few of his friends squeezed through the crowd to where Grace and Aidan were standing. "Hi, Mum. Aidan."

"Hi, Honey. Have you seen your grandmother anywhere? She should be here by now. I think I'll text her."

Jimmy looked at Aidan and then at his mother. "You haven't seen them?"

"No. We haven't seen either of them."

"Oh. Well, don't look now. Here they come."

"They?"

Aidan saw them first. "I hate to say it, but I told you so."

Grace saw them making their way through the crowd. "What the…"

"Hi, Dad. Janet."

"Hello, Son." Donald reached for Grace's hand. "Nice to see you again Grace."

Grace could barely speak. "Mr. McRae. Good to see you. Mom. Why didn't you tell us you were coming together? You could have come with us."

"It was easier to come straight from the restaurant."

Grace was confused. "Restaurant?"

"Yes. Donald took me to the Black Rock for dinner."

Aidan had to look the other way so Grace wouldn't see the grin on his face.

"The Black Rock?"

"Yes. The place you and Aidan went last night. Both of us have wanted to go there since it opened. It was great."

Grace was pulling herself together. "We liked it too, didn't we Aidan?"

"Yes. Food's great. Beautiful views. Very romantic."

Grace elbowed him.

"Grace, I don't believe Donald has met your friends."

"Oh, I'm sorry, Mr. McRae. This is Jonathan Blake and his friend Charlene Carter. I think you know Valerie. Oh, and my son, Jimmy. Everyone, this is Aidan's dad, Donald McRae."

Donald shook Jonathan's hand and nodded to the others. "Please, call me Donald. You're the writer. I've read most of your books. Jimmy, it's wonderful to see you. I'd love it if you'd come by and visit before you go back to school."

"I'll do that."

The alarm sounded. The fireworks were about to begin. Jonathan stood behind Charlene. He slid his arms around her waist. Aidan put one arm around Grace and held her against him. Together, they all watched the magnificent display. The crowd oohed and ahhed as every new burst of color lit up the blackened sky.

Grace saw Jonathan give Charlene a kiss. *Maybe he's finally met the right one.* She looked up at Aidan. She wondered what he was thinking seeing Charlene with Jonathan. He looked down at her and smiled. When she smiled back at him, Aidan hugged her tighter. She didn't know how they would work out the long distance between them, but when he kissed her in front of everyone, just before the grand finale, she was sure they would do fine.

Val looked at all of them. *Talk about your fifth wheel.* She saw Janet move a little closer to Donald. He discreetly took her hand. *How sweet is that? I gotta get a date for next year.*

CHAPTER 59
GRACE AND ELISE

When they got back to Grace's house, the lights were on in the den and Brian's truck was in the driveway. Val headed straight to her car. "Good night everyone. See you all tomorrow. I'll bring the chicken wings."

Aidan hugged Charlene. Jonathan gave Grace a hug and a quick kiss. The two men shook hands. "Charlene and I will be here around noon. Good night."

Aidan walked Grace to the front door. They could hear the TV. "I don't think I should come in. Elise is still up. I'll let you have some time with her. Besides, I'm exhausted. It's been a long day."

Grace understood. "You should get some sleep. Tomorrow will be busy."

"I'll text you in the morning to make sure you're up before I call."

"I need a good night's sleep too, but I'll be up early."

He kissed her and stood holding her for several minutes. "You better go before we both fall asleep in the doorway."

He kissed her one more time. "See you tomorrow. I love you Gracie."

"I love you too. Careful driving home."

Elise and Brian were in the den. "Hi, Mom. Where is everybody?"

"They went home."

"Aidan too?"

"He's tired."

"Hey, Mrs. Madden. How were the fireworks?"

"Wonderful. Crowded, as usual."

"Now that you're home, I'm gonna get goin'. I'm glad you're feeling better, Elise. I'll see myself out."

"Thanks for staying with me, Brian. See you tomorrow."

"I'll be here early. Jimmy and I will get the ice."

Elise looked back at her mother. "Did Gran find you?"

"She sure did."

"What do you mean?"

Grace put one hand on her hip. "Your grandmother was there with a date."

Elise's mouth flew open. "No kidding!"

"I wouldn't joke about a thing like that."

"It's not like she's never been on a date."

"She was with Donald McRae."

"Aidan's dad?"

"Yes."

"So what's the problem? You like him don't you?"

"Well, yes, but…"

"But, what?"

"I don't know exactly."

"Wasn't it her idea to invite him to the cookout?"

"Yes."

Elise was getting a kick out of her mother's reaction. "That should have told you something."

Grace sat down on the sofa. "I thought she was trying to make Aidan feel more comfortable."

"Mom. Really?"

"Aidan thought there was more to it."

Elise tapped a finger on her chin. "Gee, if they got married, Aidan would be your step-brother."

"Elise! Don't even think it. That would be terrible."

"Careful, Mom. You're starting to sound like me."

At that, mother and daughter laughed out loud.

Elise sat down next to Grace. "I've missed these mother-daughter talks."

Grace smiled. "Me too."

Elise's expression changed to a serious one. "I meant it, Mom. I'm sorry for all the trouble I've caused. I've been taking my grief out on you and blaming you for things that weren't your fault. I forgot you were hurting too."

"I do understand, Elise. I lost my father too. I guess it doesn't matter how old you are, it's hard to see your mother with someone new. I want my mother to be happy. She looked very happy tonight with Donald."

"I want you to be happy too. And, it looks to me like Aidan does that for you."

"He does, Honey."

Elise got up and threw her arms around her mother. Grace hugged her for a long time. "It's good to have my daughter back."

CHAPTER 60
AIDAN AND DONALD

It was a little after eight when Aidan stepped out of the shower. The smell of bacon drifting up the stairs made him think of his mother. He could almost hear her calling up to him. "Aidan, hurry up. Your eggs are getting cold."

Needing coffee, he dressed in a hurry and went downstairs. His dad was at the stove.

"Mornin' Sleepyhead. Eggs'll be ready shortly."

"Thanks. I don't know what happened. I rarely sleep past six. Yesterday must have caught up with me."

"Don't imagine you have such excitement in Maine."

Aidan poured himself a cup of coffee. "We have crime. I'm used to reading about it in the papers though, not participating."

His father placed a plate of bacon on the table. "I'm sure it'll make tomorrow's front page."

Aidan shook his head. "Just what Elise needs."

"Young people are resilient."

Aidan changed the subject. "Do I dare ask how your date went last night?"

Donald brought their eggs over and sat down. "Great restaurant. I wasn't disappointed."

"I wasn't talking about the restaurant."

"Neither was I."

Aidan looked across the table. "You old dog."

His dad chuckled. "Just havin' some fun with you. I was a perfect gentleman."

"I knew that."

"Janet's a nice woman. We have a lot in common."

"Why didn't you tell me you were going out with her last night?"

"It was spur of the moment. Frank called me about what happened with you. I thought she might want to be there for Grace. I called her. We got talking. Next thing I knew, I had a dinner date."

Aidan smiled at his dad. "I'm glad you had a good time. Thanks for making breakfast."

Aidan checked his phone. Seeing Grace's text, he called her.

"Good morning."

"Hi! How are you feeling? Did you sleep well?"

"Like a rock. I feel great. We just finished breakfast. How's Elise?"

"Much better. We had a long talk last night. She was shaken by what happened. It made her realize what's important to her. It also changed the way she's been feeling about you. She's looking forward to the cookout."

"I'm glad. Have you talked to your mother this morning?"

"No. She's busy making potato salad. Thought I'd leave her alone, since she may have been out late last night. She'll be over in a while."

"I don't think it was all that late. I heard my dad come in shortly after I went to bed."

"I don't know why they kept it a secret. They could have come with us."

"Honey, they're adults. Maybe they didn't feel the need for chaperones."

Grace laughed. "You're right."

"I'll bring the steak tips when I come. Anything else you need?"

"No. I think everything's covered. Even the weather is cooperating. It's supposed to be hot, but not humid."

"Can't ask for more than that. What time do you want me there?"

"Come whenever you like. Val and Mom will be here by noon. Not sure about Jonathan and Charlene. The guests start showing up around one. You and Jonathan can help Jimmy with the cooking. We start the grills about two."

"Sounds good. I'll be over by eleven." Aidan got another cup of coffee and joined his dad on the porch. It felt good to be home.

CHAPTER 61
THE COOKOUT

When Aidan arrived, Jimmy and Brian had stocked the coolers and gone for ice. Elise was in the kitchen making the salad. "Come on in. Mom's in the basement getting wine."

He put the steak tips on the counter. "A little early, isn't it?"

She laughed. "She'll make room for that when she comes up. Thanks for not asking how I'm doing? I know people are concerned, but I'm trying not to think about it."

He understood. "They mean well, but you have to relive it every time someone brings it up."

"I imagine you're getting the same thing."

"Yeah, but not many people around here have my phone number."

"Aidan. I thought I heard you come in." Grace came through the door with a bottle of white wine in her hands. She walked over and kissed him. "I'm glad you're here. Can I get you anything?"

"Not just yet, thanks, " Aidan teased.

She didn't get the joke. "What? Oh, this is for later. I want to put it in the cooler. Jimmy forgot to bring it up."

Aidan looked over his shoulder and gave Elise a wink. "I'm all set for now."

Grace put the tips in the fridge and made room for the salad and potato salad. The boys came back with the ice. Aidan helped them put it in the coolers. Janet walked into the yard carrying a huge foil covered bowl. He went over and took it out of her hands.

"Let me help you with that."

"Thank you. It's heavy."

Janet followed him into the kitchen. "You seem to have things under control, as usual Grace. The yard looks great."

"Thanks. I had a lot of help."

"Good morning, Elise. You're looking much better today."

Elise hugged and kissed her grandmother. "Hi, Gran. I heard you had an interesting evening."

Janet made it clear she was not going to elaborate on her date. "Yes, I did."

"Can someone take these wings, please? I left something in my car. Elise, Daphne and her boyfriend just got here."

Grace hurried over to Val. "I'll take them."

Jonathan and Charlene were right behind her, each carrying a white box. "Where would you like these pastries? Charlene brought them from the bakery you liked in Maine."

"Over on the counter is fine. Thank you, Charlene."

Jonathan hugged all the women and shook Aidan's hand. "I didn't see Jimmy out there."

Elise giggled. "He went to pick up Priscilla."

"Who's Priscilla?"

"Someone he met at school. She lives in Salem. We haven't met her yet."

Jonathan raised his eyebrows. "A law student? Way to go, Jim. Ladies, I'm gonna leave Charlene in here with you for now." He turned toward Aidan. "How 'bout a beer before they put us to work?"

"Sounds good." He followed Jonathan outside.

Charlene turned toward Grace. "I want to thank you again for inviting me. I had a wonderful time yesterday and the fireworks were terrific. Funny how things work out sometimes, isn't it?"

"Yes. Life's full of surprises. That day at the bookstore, who ever thought the four of us would be together like this today?"

"I have to say, Aidan looks very happy."

Looking out the window, Grace knew she'd be seeing a lot more of Charlene. "So does Jonathan."

The two men were sitting at one of the umbrella tables. Jonathan put his beer down and faced Aidan. "I really like Charlene. I want you to know that."

"I'd say she feels the same way about you. I know you weren't too keen on the idea of Grace and me."

"That was stupidity on my part and, I'll admit, a little jealousy. But, anyone can see how you two feel about each other."

Aidan was feeling better about Jonathan. He hoped things worked out between him and Charlene. "We're a couple of lucky guys."

Jonathan raised his bottle and touched it to Aidan's. "That we are. The four of us should get together for dinner soon. Maybe when Grace is in Maine."

"Good idea. We could all spend a day at the lake and then go to dinner."

"I'm sure the ladies would love it. We can let them plan it. Oh, here comes your dad."

Jonathan stood up and greeted Donald. "Good to see you again."

Janet came out of the house and walked up to where they were standing. "I hope those are marinated mushrooms you're carrying."

He handed her the covered container and gave her a quick kiss on the cheek. "I wouldn't dare show up without them."

"Hi, Dad. I'll let Janet introduce you around."

"I think he knows just about everyone here, but I'll make sure. Let's bring these in the house and then we'll get you a beer." Donald gave his son a thumbs up and followed Janet.

A few heads turned when Jimmy walked in with Priscilla. She was tall and slender. In sandals, she came up past his shoulder. He introduced her to Jonathan and Aidan before taking the shapely, blue-eyed blonde in the house to meet his family. Once she was sufficiently overwhelmed, he brought her back outside to meet his friends.

The women brought out appetizers as the guests started to arrive. Jonathan finished his beer. "I think that's our cue to start the grills."

He went over to Jimmy and pulled him aside. "Listen, Jim, I don't want you to think I'm trying to take over or anything, but if you want to spend some time with your friend, Aidan and I can handle the cooking."

Jimmy looked relieved. "You sure you don't mind? She doesn't know anyone. I kind of hate to leave her alone that long."

"No problem. Besides, it will give me a chance to get to know Aidan better."

Jonathan went back to the table where Aidan was still sitting. "It's you and me, buddy. I thought Jim might not want to leave his date unattended."

Aidan laughed. "Good idea. You light the grills. I'll tell Grace to start bringing out the food. I'm gonna get a lemonade. You want anything?"

"Another beer would be good."

The guests were enjoying the appetizers and perfect weather. Some of Jimmy's friends were in the pool. Elise and Brian sat with Daphne and her date and a few others. Aidan was happy to be cooking. It kept him away from the crowd.

Charlene helped Grace and Val bring out the food. She handed Aidan his steak tips. "These are yours. I could tell."

"Don't all steak tips look alike?"

"Yeah, but Donald told me you made these. How's it going out here?"

"Very funny. We're doing good. We've been talking about the four of us spending a day at the lake and goin' to dinner."

"Really? That would be fantastic. I'm so glad you and Jonathan are getting to know each other."

"So am I. He's not a bad guy."

When they were finished cooking, Jonathan and Aidan joined Grace and Charlene. Jonathan complimented Grace on the food. "Everything is delicious."

"You and Aidan cooked it."

"In that case, my compliments to the chefs."

When they were done eating, Jonathan went inside and cut up the watermelon. Charlene and Grace brought out the pastries and desserts.

As the guests consumed more alcohol, the noise level in the yard increased. It made Aidan anxious. The loud voices and high-pitched squeals from the girls in the pool were getting on his nerves. He needed to get away from the crowd for a while. Grace was talking to Priscilla. He worked his way to the back door and slipped into the kitchen.

CHAPTER 62
AIDAN AND ELISE

Aidan could still hear the clamor coming from the yard. *I just need a little peace and quiet for a while.* He walked through the kitchen to the den. As he was about to sit down, he noticed Elise curled up on the recliner. "I'm sorry. I didn't realize you were in here." Not wanting to disturb her, he turned to walk out.

"It's okay. You don't have to leave."

"Are you sure? If you want to be alone, I understand."

"I needed to get out of the noise for a while. I had some thinking to do. This was my dad's chair. I like sitting here. It makes me feel close to him somehow. Does that sound silly?"

What she said made him feel melancholy. "Not at all. I feel like that about the kitchen at my dad's house. I sit at the table and picture my mom standing in front of the sink washing dishes. I can smell her fresh baked cookies in that room sometimes."

"Is that what you were doing at the cemetery yesterday? Visiting your mom?"

"I always stop by to see her when I come home."

"Does it get any easier? Missing them?"

Aidan had seen the same painful look in Kelli's eyes many times. He sat on the couch across from her. "I wish I could tell you it does. All I can say is, you learn to cope with the pain in time. But, it never goes away. You never stop missing them. At least, that's how it is for me."

"My dad sat in this chair and read the paper every night after work."

"You like to come in here and think about him. There's nothing wrong with that. Hang on to your memories, Elise. Just don't let them stop you from living your life. Your dad wouldn't want that to happen."

"I guess that's what I've been doing."

"You know, you're lucky in a strange way."

His comment confused her. "What do you mean?"

"You have so many good memories of your dad. My daughter barely remembers her mother."

"You lost your wife?"

"No. We were divorced when Kelli was two. She was six years old when her mom died in an accident."

Elise had forgotten her mother mentioned Aidan raised his daughter alone. "So she doesn't remember a lot about her mom then."

"No. And I don't have a lot of memories to give her. I didn't know Maryann that long myself. All she has is a photo album with whatever pictures I could scrape together and a few pieces of jewelry that belonged to her mother."

"You raised her by yourself? You never re-married?"

"No. I never married again."

"I'm sorry. I probably shouldn't have asked that question."

"It's okay. I don't mind."

Elise leaned forward and looked at Aidan. "I'm sure my mom told you about the letter I found in her office. An old letter from you. I didn't read the whole thing. That's the truth."

He believed her. "But, you read enough to assume things?"

"I read enough to realize her book was about you and that you were in love with my mother back then."

Aidan thought he should be honest with her. "I loved her then and I love her now."

"After all those years."

"Elise, your mother loved your father. They had a good life together. She has no regrets about that. She misses him as much as you do. I can't talk about what happened or why I left, but it's important for you to know I had no contact with her until the day I went to the bookstore and she had no idea I was going to be there."

"I believe you."

He smiled and stood up. "Good. Now, I think I've interrupted your alone time long enough."

Elise stood up too. She put her hand on his arm. "Aidan, wait. I have something else I need to say to you."

He was almost afraid of what else she wanted to know. "All right."

"I never got to thank you for what you did yesterday."

"There's no need to thank me."

"Yes, there is. But, first, I want to tell you I'm sorry I caused so much trouble. I hope you can forgive me."

Aidan could have forgiven her anything when she looked at him with those green eyes that were so much like Grace. "There's nothing to forgive. It's all behind us now."

Her smile was genuine. "Thank you for that. And, thank you for yesterday. You put yourself in danger to help me. I'll never forget it."

"I'm sure if he hadn't knocked you down, you would have gotten to him before I did."

"I doubt it." Elise gave Aidan a hug. "Now I'm ready to go back outside."

CHAPTER 63
THE WRAP UP

Grace was about to go inside to check on Aidan when she saw him coming out of the house with Elise.

"There you are. Brian's been looking for you. Everything okay?"

Elise smiled at Aidan. "Everything's fine." She hugged her mother. "You two enjoy the rest of the cookout. I'd better go find Brian."

Grace gave Aidan a puzzled look. "What was that all about?"

"Your daughter and I just had a nice long talk."

"You and Elise? What about?"

He took Grace by the hand and led her to a quiet corner of the yard. "She apologized for the way she's been acting and thanked me for yesterday."

"She did? Oh, Aidan, I'm so happy to hear that."

"We talked about how it feels to lose a parent. We have that in common. I told her about Kelli and what it's been like for her without a mom."

Grace knew that must have been a difficult subject for Aidan to discuss.

"She brought up the letter. I set her straight on the misguided notion she had that you and I were together while Jim was alive. I'm sure she saw me as a threat."

Grace didn't understand. "A threat? How?"

"She was afraid her life would change if you got married again."

"Married! How did she ever get that far ahead with all this? I should have tried harder to make her understand."

"Don't go blaming yourself. Elise has to learn to take responsibility for her own actions. She backed herself into a corner and couldn't find a way out. What happened yesterday scared her. It made her realize how much her family means to her and that she can always count on her mother. She seems okay with you and me now. I was honest with her. I told her how I feel about you."

"Do you really think everything will be all right now?"

He leaned over and kissed her cheek. "More than all right."

Grace tended to her guests for the rest of the afternoon, making sure everyone was having a good time. Aidan was tired of hashing over the incident in the cemetery. Charlene noticed him standing alone in a corner of the yard. Knowing how he felt about crowds, she went over to him.

"You look like you've had enough partying. Come sit with us. J B and I are planning another author event for sometime near the end of July."

Grateful for the rescue, he grabbed a bottle of lemonade out of the cooler and followed her to the umbrella table. "Maybe we can schedule a day at the lake and dinner at the same time. I'm sure Grace will come up for the book signing anyway."

"That's a great idea."

Jonathan agreed. "We could have the event on a Thursday or Friday, so we can come to your place on a Saturday, unless during the week works better for the two of you. I know you'll both have to consider coverage for your businesses."

"I can be pretty flexible. As long as I know far enough in advance, Sam can cover the store."

"I can usually take a day off without a problem too. It's a little more difficult to take off on a Saturday though."

Jonathan pulled out a notebook and a pen. "Let's write down a couple of possible dates and then check with Grace."

As the guests started to leave, Aidan and Jonathan helped the boys fold chairs and clean up the yard. The women brought in the food and cleaned the kitchen. By seven o'clock, the neighbors had all gone.

"I'm taking Priscilla home now, Mum. We'll probably stop at her uncle's. Don't wait up."

"Good night, Mrs. Madden, Mr. McRae. It was nice meeting both of you. I had a great time."

"We enjoyed having you. Thank you for helping in the kitchen."

Jimmy shook Aidan's hand. "Thanks for helping with the grills. See you soon."

"Glad to help, Jim. Hope you'll bring Priscilla up to the lake while you're home."

Donald walked over to Grace and Aidan. "I put Janet's table in my car. I'll follow her home and get it in the house."

He took Grace's hands in his. "Thank you for inviting me. I had a wonderful time."

"Thank you for coming. Hope we'll be seeing more of you."

He laughed and looked across the yard at Janet. "Oh, I'm sure you will be. I thought it would be nice if the four of us could have breakfast together tomorrow before Aidan leaves. I already asked your mother. Aidan and I will do the cooking."

Aidan shrugged his shoulders and smiled. "Don't look at me. I didn't know anything about it, but I think it's a great idea."

Grace smiled at Donald. "I'd love to come."

"By the way, Janet and I are taking a ride to Gloucester tomorrow. We'll be leaving right after breakfast, but you two take your time. Have a second cup of coffee if you want. Stay as long as you like. We'll be gone until late in the afternoon. You'll have the house to yourselves."

Grace saw the wink he gave Aidan. She could feel her face turning red.

"Don't worry about us, Dad. You and Janet enjoy your day."

"Did I hear my name mentioned?" Janet took Donald's arm. "Are we all on for breakfast?"

Aidan was glad she interrupted before his dad said anything else. "We're all set."

"I'm ready when you are, Donald. It was a great cookout, Grace. Good night, Aidan. We'll see both of you in the morning."

Grace looked up at Aidan. "Did he mean what I think he meant?"

"I'm sorry if he embarrassed you. He likes to play Cupid."

"That's okay. I'm looking forward to that second cup of coffee after they leave."

"Mom, Brian and I are going over to Daphne's. I won't be too late."

"Okay, Elise. Thank you for all your help, Brian."

Elise hugged both of them and followed Brian out of the yard.

Aidan looked forward to having Grace all to himself for a couple of hours. He wanted to hold her close and tell her how much she meant to him.

Jonathan interrupted his thoughts. "You guys about done out here? Charlene and I will be leaving soon. Come have coffee with us before we go. Val made a fresh pot."

Aidan turned toward Jonathan. "We'll be right there."

He waited for him to go back in the house. The yard was finally empty. Aidan wrapped his arms around Grace and kissed her the way he did standing by his truck that day in Perkins Cove.

"Now, we can have coffee."

CHAPTER 64
BREAKFAST

Grace picked her mother up on the way to Donald's for breakfast.

"Thanks for picking me up. Donald can drop me off when we come back from Gloucester. We won't have to worry about two cars."

"No problem. Just put those pastries in the back. I wanted to bring something. I had a lot of leftovers."

"I can keep them on my lap. We don't have far to go. It was a good party. The whole weekend was great. The fireworks were the best I've seen in years."

Grace couldn't help smiling at her mother. "You think maybe the company had something to do with it?"

Janet glanced over at her daughter. "Didn't you think the fireworks were fantastic?"

"Of course. But, watching them with Aidan made them better for me. That's all I meant."

Janet knew exactly what she meant. "I know what you're thinking."

"What?"

"That your mother dating your boyfriend's father is a bit weird."

"Are you and Donald dating? I mean, is that what you call it?"

"What do you call dinner at the Black Rock and fireworks, a coincidence? He's cooking my breakfast and taking me to Gloucester for the day. Yes, Grace, we call it dating at our age, too."

Grace had to admit it did feel strange. "I'm sorry. Okay. It does seem a little weird."

"Wait until word of this gets around. Marion Munford is going to be fuming."

"What business is it of hers?"

"She's been after Donald McRae since the day they buried poor Emma. Far as I know, he's never given her the time of day, but she still chases after him. When she hears his car was in my driveway until eleven o'clock last night, it will be the talk of her art group and all over the senior center. She volunteers there too."

"How would she find out?"

"Her best friend lives across the street from me."

Grace didn't like the thought of her mother being gossiped about. "Well, I think it's wonderful. He's a very nice man. You seem to get along well. It's none of her business or anyone else's for that matter."

"I've gone out on dates before, you know. But, Donald and I have a lot in common. He loves to garden and he's a good cook. I enjoy his company and love his sense of humor. He's handsome too and likes to go on day trips. The hell with Marion."

The two women laughed the rest of the way.

When they arrived, Donald was standing on the porch. "Good morning, ladies."

Janet commented on his flowers. "Good morning. Your Daisies look so cheerful in the sunlight."

"Thank you." He stopped to show her the other pots. "Aidan's in the kitchen, Grace. Go on in."

Grace opened the screen door and stepped inside. He was pouring milk into a pitcher. "Coffee smells good." She placed the pastry on the counter. "Brought you something sweet."

He smiled, put the milk down and gave her more than a warm welcome. "So you did."

Neither of them heard the door open.

Donald cleared his throat. "I think the coffee's ready."

Aidan quickly pulled away from Grace and snapped to attention. "Sorry. Good morning, Janet."

He poured them all coffee.

Donald walked over to the stove. "I'll take it from here. You sit and talk to our guests."

Aidan filled a plate with pastry and brought it over to the table.

"I hope you enjoyed the cookout Aidan, even though my daughter put you to work for most of the weekend."

"Yes, I did. Thank you."

He looked at Grace. "Those were some fireworks after everyone went home last night."

Janet dropped her spoon. Donald spun around and looked at Aidan.

When Aidan realized how that sounded, he attempted to explain. "We watched the Boston Pops and the fireworks on TV after everyone left."

Donald shook his head and went back to cooking the bacon. *Good save, Aidan.*

Janet took a long sip of her coffee. "Boston always puts on a beautiful display."

Grace changed the subject. "So…you two are going to Gloucester for the day. That sounds like fun."

"We both like to take day trips. Donald suggested Gloucester for our first one."

Grace was glad her mother found someone to do things with. "There are so many interesting places not far from here. Newburyport, Portsmouth, Boston."

Aidan got up to help Donald serve the food. "There's also Cape Cod, if you don't mind the traffic."

Donald handed him the bacon. "We might take a ride to Ogunquit next week. They have a lot of good restaurants there, if my memory serves me right."

Aidan winked at Grace. "Grace and I spent a day in Ogunquit recently. She took me to dinner there. We can give you a few good suggestions."

Janet hadn't seen her daughter this happy in a long time. Aidan looked happy too. She had reservations about a romance between them at first, but now, she could see how much they love each other and believed they could make it work.

"That's good to know. I'll check with Grace before we go."

When they finished breakfast, Janet got up and started clearing the table.

Aidan took the dishes from her. "Grace and I will do that. You two need to get on the road."

"You go on, Mom. Don't worry about the dishes."

Donald gave Aidan a hug. "Been nice having you home. Maybe Janet and I will come visit you soon."

"I'd like that very much, Dad."

"We'll get our things and be on our way. Grace, I'm sure I'll see you soon."

She gave Donald a hug and a kiss on the cheek. "Yes. You have fun today."

They cleared the table and walked out to the porch with Janet and Donald. Aidan put his arm around Grace. The two of them watched the car turn the corner and disappear.

"Why do I feel like I did when Elise went off on her first date?"

"They say the children become the parents."

He wanted to kiss her, but not on the front porch of his father's house. "Let's go inside. I'll show you my room."

Laughing, she followed him into the house. "You're not supposed to have girls in your room when there's no parent home."

Aidan slipped his arms around Grace's waist, pulled her close and kissed her. The warmth of her lips excited him. "We're the parents, remember?"

She wrapped her arms around his neck and looked up at him. Her emerald eyes danced in the sunlight that streamed through the kitchen window.

"I love you, Aidan."

"I love you, Gracie."

She had no more doubts. "We're going to make this work. I believe that now."

He leaned down to kiss her again.

"I've always believed it."

Dear Readers:

Thank you for reading *Loving Daniel*, the first book in my *Tucker's Landing Series*. Watch for Jonathan's story in book two, *Worth Waiting For*.

Here's a preview.

Lina

WORTH WAITING FOR

CHAPTER 1
JONATHAN

Jonathan held the one and a half karat solitaire between his thumb and forefinger. It sparkled in the sunlight that streamed through the window of his den. He placed it back in the blue velvet box, punched in the code to his wall safe and tucked it way in the back. *It's just going to have to wait, for now.*

He sat down at his desk and called Charlene.

"J B! You haven't left yet?"

His voice was shaky. "No, Honey...my sister called. I... have to go to Albany."

She was afraid to ask. "Is it your dad?"

"Ya...he's had another heart attack. Amanda says it doesn't look good. I have to leave right away."

"Jonathan, I'm so sorry. Is there anything I can do?"

"Pray that he makes it."

Charlene wanted to comfort him in person. Doing it long distance was difficult. "I will. Tell Amanda and your mom I'm thinking of them. I wish I could give you a hug. Living so far apart has its disadvantages."

Jonathan thought about what he had planned for this weekend before he got the phone call. "We need to work on that. I have to go. I love you."

"I love you, too, J B. Drive carefully. Keep me posted."

Jonathan slipped his phone into his shirt pocket and went upstairs to finish packing. He added three dress shirts and two neckties to his suitcase. Taking the diamond tie tac out of his jewelry box made him think about the ring. He remembered the last time he gave someone an engagement ring. *What a bad idea that turned out to be.* He closed the suitcase, lifted it off the bed, got his dark blue suit out of the closet and headed back downstairs. After carrying them out to his car, he went back in, grabbed his laptop, locked up the house and left.

On the drive to Albany, he thought about his last conversation with his dad. He was the only one Jonathan told about his marriage plans.

"I couldn't be happier, Son. Your mother and I love Charlene."

He smiled at his father's approval. "Thanks, Dad. She loves you too. You think she'll say yes?"

"Of course she'll say yes!" Henry Blake boomed into the phone. "The woman loves you. Anyone can see that. I imagine you'll move to Maine, since she has a business and a son there."

"That's what I'm figuring. I can write anywhere. I can't expect her to give up her bookstore and move to Tucker's Landing."

"I gave up hoping you'd come back to Albany a long time ago. But, I'm happy you've made a nice life for yourself. As long as you come to visit, I can't complain."

"Don't tell Mom yet, okay. I want to keep it under wraps until there's an announcement to be made."

"I won't say anything, but your mother will be thrilled. She's always wanted to see you settle down. She never liked that actress you were engaged to, you know. For that matter, neither did I. She just wasn't the right girl for you. But, we didn't want to interfere."

"I know, Dad. I appreciated it. It took me a long time, but I finally found the right one."

"Good luck, Son. Talk to you soon. I love you."

"Love you too, Dad."

Jonathan didn't want to think about Nikki King, the beautiful young actress with the honey blonde hair and sultry brown eyes he'd fallen in love with, over fifteen years ago. He left Albany shortly after she broke off their two-year engagement. The last he heard, she moved to Beverly Hills. According to the tabloids, she'd been married and divorced twice and was working on number three.

That was in the past. Now, he had a wonderful woman who loved him. One he could trust and count on. Charlene Carter wasn't flamboyant or hung up on herself. She was a thoughtful, caring person, a good mother and a smart businesswoman. *Finding her is the best thing that ever happened to me.*

ABOUT THE AUTHOR

Lina Rehal is a self-published author and freelance writer known for her short stories, nostalgic pieces and newspaper features. By combining her passion for fiction and love of storytelling, she has found a new voice in writing romance novels.

Loving Daniel is the first in a series about Tucker's Landing, a small coastal town in Massachusetts. She is currently working on book two, *Worth Waiting For*.

Lina lives north of Boston with her husband. When not writing, she enjoys time with her family, creating stories with her ten-year-old granddaughter and trips to New Hampshire, Maine and Disneyworld.

She is the founder and facilitator of North Shore Scribes, a member of Romance Writers of America and The Red Rock Rewriters. Her first two books are available on Amazon.com and Kindle. Carousel Kisses is a collection of personal essays and poems about growing up in the late 1950's to early 1960's. Her second book, October In New York is a novella and her first published romance story.

She loves hearing from readers. You may contact Lina through her website or email.

Contact Lina Rehal

Email: rehalcute@aol.com

Website

www.thefuzzypinkmuse.com

Made in United States
North Haven, CT
03 March 2024